The Highland Countess

The Highland Countess

Marion Chesney

G.K. Hall & Co. • Chivers Press
Thorndike, Maine USA   Bath, England

This Large Print edition is published by G.K. Hall & Co., USA
and by Chivers Press, England.

Published in 1999 in the U.S. by arrangement with Signet,
a division of Penguin Putnam Inc.

Published in 1999 in the U.K. by arrangement with Marion Chesney.

U.S. Softcover   0-7838-8740-X (Paperback Series Edition)
U.K. Hardcover 0-7540-3953-6 (Chivers Large Print)
U.K. Softcover   0-7540-3954-4 (Camden Large Print)

The text of this Large Print edition is unabridged.
Other aspects of the book may vary from the original edition.

Set in 16 pt. Plantin by Juanita Macdonald.

Printed in the United States on permanent paper.

British Library Cataloguing-in-Publication Data available

Library of Congress Cataloging-in-Publication Data

Chesney, Marion.
    The Highland countess / Marion Chesney.
        p.   cm.
    ISBN 0-7838-8740-X (lg. print : sc : alk. paper)
    1. Large type books.   I. Title.
  PR6053.H4535H54   1999
    823´.914—dc21   99-37951

For
Howard Lewis

Chapter One

The newly wed Countess of Murr had not, as yet, read any novels or poetry and she had not — as yet — fallen in love . . . which was perhaps just as well.

Morag had celebrated her seventeenth birthday shortly before her wedding to the earl. The earl was fifty-four. She was a true Highland beauty with thick, curly, dark-red hair and a creamy complexion. There are two types of redheads in Scotland. One is the more sandy-haired variety which goes with a pale, freckled complexion and light eyelashes. The second category, to which Morag belonged, has hair of a red which is almost purple in tone and has all the beauty of a flawless complexion and vivid eyes.

Her eyes were of a particularly intense blue and were fringed with heavy black lashes. Such notables as His Grace, the Duke of Wellington, might consider red hair "unfortunate" and go so far as to shave his son's eyebrows in an attempt to mitigate some of the unsightly color, but Morag was still far from the hot drawing rooms of London, and, in Perthshire, Scotland, where she was in the process of settling into her new married life, her hair was considered a thing of beauty.

Two weeks after her marriage, she was pacing the castle gardens and wondering uneasily if all marriages were like hers.

Her father, the Laird of Clacharder, had kept her well away from any young men, and his few servants were old. Her sole companion had been her English governess, a gaunt female called Miss Simpson who taught Morag her prunes and prisms and use of the globes and imposed on Morag's natural, soft, Scottish burr the arctic and glacial tones of the upper-class English. Morag's mother had died when she was a baby and she had no other female to advise her.

She had assumed, however, that one day she would make her come-out at the balls and assemblies of Edinburgh like other young females of her class. But her father had other plans. One day he had abruptly told her that she was betrothed to the Earl of Murr. Morag did not consider for a moment disobeying her father, though it all seemed very strange. No dream knight cantered to her rescue across the virginal fields of her mind. After all, a steady diet of sermons and judicious extracts from the Bible was hardly conducive to romance.

Great clouds tugged across the sky above the battlements of the castle driven by a high wind, but not a breeze whispered over the high walls of the castle gardens where the air was warm and still.

Morag sat down on a marble bench — feet together, back straight as a ramrod — and stared unseeingly at the riot of color around her: roses, dahlias, lupine, gladioli and fuchsia. Her marriage was not an ordinary one, of that she was becoming increasingly sure. She went over the events of the wedding and after in an effort to clarify her thoughts.

The bewilderment had started when her father, Angus Grant, had sent Miss Simpson to her on her wedding morn with instructions to "put a few of the facts of life into the lassie's head."

Like marriage, the facts of life had escaped Miss Simpson. She had been born to one of the laird's father's tenant farmers. Her father had been proud of his clever daughter and had had her educated at the local school. She had obtained a post as governess to the English Marquess of Devizes and had traveled south to make her fortune. But after having worked for forty years in various titled households, she had found herself too old to find another post in the fickle south, and so she had returned to her native land. The laird had offered her room and board, provided she acted as companion and governess to his daughter, Morag, and she had gratefully accepted, her father being now dead and her brother who had inherited the farm having a shrew of a wife.

Nonetheless, spinster though she was, she had often overheard strange and disturbing conversations in her sojourn in England. So she tried her best.

"There are some things, Miss Grant," said the governess, turning an interesting shade of mottled purple, "that a young girl should know about her wedding night."

"Oh," said Morag, trying to give the governess her full attention while coping with novel feelings of excitement and anticipation. She had never been away from home before. Now she would have a house of her own — and a castle at that.

"Yes," went on Miss Simpson, faint but pursuing. "You will share a bed with your lord and he will do things to you that are necessary to beget a child."

Now Miss Simpson had Morag's full blue-eyed attention. "What things?"

"Things that a young lady does not discuss or even think about," said Miss Simpson, breathing hard. "You must simply endure whatever happens, close your eyes tightly and think of the king."

Miss Simpson avoided Morag's eyes, staring at some point over the girl's shoulder. Morag did not know that Miss Simpson had heard several unsavory stories about the earl — that although he had been married before, he had no legitimate heir, only a string of bastards, and that he could only take his pleasures with the lowest of the serving wenches but that a high-bred lady "froze his balls" — an expression which Miss

10

Simpson did not understand, thinking it referred to some heraldic term or something like the ball and sceptre. But deep in her heart, Miss Simpson envied Morag. Who was ever happily married anyway? A husband meant a secure future for a woman. Morag would never know what it meant to be passed from household to household.

"Age," said Miss Simpson grimly, tucking a stray strand of gray hair under her starched cap, "must always be honored. Remember what I have said."

But Morag merely stroked the satin sheen of her wedding gown and thought of her fine trousseau and forgot, for the moment, everything the governess had said.

Her lord, the Earl of Murr, indeed looked old when she first saw him, which was in front of the altar, although he seemed like a resplendent figure of a man with his great chest, slim hips and good legs with fine calves. His eyes, which were as blue as Morag's own, were slightly bulbous and his mouth was loose and wet, but he had a fine head of nut-brown hair.

Morag had trained herself to enjoy the best of each minute no matter what the circumstances. It was her way of combating the loneliness of her solitary life. So she simply enjoyed the feel of the new clothes against her body, the fine dresses of the wedding guests and the fact that her father, who hardly ever seemed to notice her, was actually shedding sentimental tears.

The journey from her home among the grim mountains of the Highlands was too uncomfortable and fatiguing to allow for any dalliance, so no attempt at consummating the marriage took place until the night of their arrival at Castle Murr.

The wedding night was very strange. It was embarrassing to sit propped against the pillows watching her husband being undressed by his valet.

First the nut-brown hair turned out to be a wig which, once removed, disclosed a nearly bald pate. Then when my lord's corsets were unlaced, his chest fell to somewhere about his knees and, furthermore, his fine calves were made of wood and came off with his stockings.

He seemed to be looking forward to his wedding night for he leaped on the bed with a triumphant cry and got to work immediately while Morag lay back, the hem of her nightgown nearly strangling her, and thought of the king. In her mind, nakedness and humiliation seemed destined to go hand in hand. Her thrashings from her father had been administered on her bare buttocks. Her wedding night began to seem like some form of equally stern chastisement, and certainly the earl was old enough to be her father. After an exhausting time, thrashing impotently about on top of her, the earl roared, "I cannae dae a thing wi' ye, ye cauld bitch. Och, ye mak me sick!"

And with that, he had heaved himself off her,

off the bed and stomped out of the room.

She had not seen him the next day, but in the evening he had once more joined her in bed with as little success as the night before.

Although life was becoming much more civilized in this new modern world of the beginning of the nineteenth century, it is probable that under these circumstances the earl would have quietly and quickly disposed of his wife. He could have openly stabbed her to death and never been brought to trial, his servants and tenants depending on him as they did for their livelihood. But fortunately for Morag, he remembered the open envy and admiration of his elderly friends and relatives at the wedding. Somewhere in a corner of his bloated soul was a true appreciation of beauty, so instead of starting off by thrashing Morag in sheer frustration, he took himself down the back stairs and was shortly exploring the buxom charms of the new scullery maid and proving to his satisfaction that he had not grown impotent with age.

The scullery maid was a willing, clever girl, quick to learn and low enough to suit his taste. Morag did not yet know that thanks to her rival she was to be allowed to sleep alone, keep her virginity and enjoy her title. Fortunately for her, the earl had decided to keep her as an ornament to show his friends — and as a weapon to use against his brother.

Virginal Morag, sitting among the blaze of

flowers in the garden, shook her head over the mysteries of marriage and decided she did not understand anything about them at all. With her optimistic nature, she put aside these troublesome thoughts and began to "count her blessings" as Miss Simpson had taught her to do.

"Firstly," thought Morag, looking about her, "it is very pretty here. Much prettier than at home." Home had been a low, square, damp barracks of a place, perched on the side of a mountain, forever dark and forever cold, with smoky peat fires burning in the winter. Despite the presence of the elderly servants, these was always a great deal of sewing and housework to do, not to mention the endless hours of study, her father being unfashionable enough to consider that a female should have a well-informed mind.

"Secondly, my husband appears to be very rich." Her own father, she knew, was quite poor, even for one of the Scottish gentry. His living came from sheep farming and his political security from his father's having changed his religion to Protestant and his allegiance to King George in time to avoid the scourge of the Highlands which had followed Prince Charles Edward Stuart's abortive rebellion. But at least neither he nor his tenants had been sent to America as slaves, a common enough punishment for Jacobites who had escaped the sword.

"Thirdly, perhaps I shall be allowed to go to Edinburgh." Morag did not have many daydreams or fantasies but she did want to see the capital city and look at the shops and see what kind of gowns the fine ladies wore and perhaps talk to young women of her own age.

The sun shifted slightly and a shadow swept across the grass at her feet. It was time to join her lord for dinner, which was served at three o'clock. He had told her gruffly that he expected her presence.

She ran lightly into the castle and, mounting to the first floor, entered the small, square, oak-paneled dining room where the earl was seated. He looked up as she entered and she dropped him a low curtsy. She was wearing an old-fashioned round gown of blue wool, but it matched the color of her eyes and her hair burned like a flame in the darkness of the room. The earl privately thought she looked breath-taking but he gave her his customary greeting, "Well, sit yerself down, ye whey-faced bitch."

Morag found nothing strange about this greeting. In just such a manner did her father address his herdsmen. "And how are you today, my lord?" she rejoined politely.

"There's a letter frae yer faither," he said, tossing over a piece of parchment, "and a wee bit in the Perthshire *Times* about the wedding. If I find the rat who wrote that rubbish, I'll hae him whipped at the cart's tail.

"Did ye ever see the like?"

Morag looked at the newspaper and blinked in surprise and delight at the description of the "beautiful Countess." Further down the reporter had written, "The Marriage of the Earl and Countess of Murr was Consummated before the Altar to the sound of the Organ."

"Very pretty," she remarked at last. "What is wrong with it?"

"God gie me patience," howled the earl. "Don't ye see anything wrong with it? Consummated, indeed!"

"Oh, yes, that . . . terrible," agreed Morag politely, inwardly vowing to look up the word *consummated* in the dictionary. "I must write to father. He will be anxious to know the details of our married life."

"Tell him," said the earl evenly, "and I'll shoot ye."

Morag's eyes clouded with confusion, then cleared. "Oh, you mean about what goes on in our bedchamber? Oh no, my lord. Miss Simpson says that a lady never talks about that."

"Quite right," said the earl, mopping his brow and wondering whether there was madness in the laird's family. He fell to studying his wife as she ate her food with a healthy appetite. Things had not worked out the way he had planned, but at least his marriage was successful to all outward appearances, and that was all that mattered. The fact that the servants must know that all was not well did not trouble him in the slightest, any more than he paused to consider the emotions of his horse.

Morag must be worn and displayed like a gem and especially to one person in particular, his

16

heir and brother, Lord Arthur Fleming.

The earl detested Lord Arthur, but the fact that Lord Arthur showed every sign of remaining his heir did not trouble the earl one whit. He did not care in the slightest what happened to his lands or title when he passed on, and anyway he felt immortal most of the time. But he had long been in the habit of competing with his young brother, and Arthur had lately become wed to a young lady of high degree who was accounted a beauty. She would pale before the glory of his Morag, thought the earl gleefully. Also, Arthur would expect a bride as young and healthy as Morag to produce heirs and that prospect should give his dear brother at least a few uncomfortable years. Arthur and his wife had been visiting London and had not been present at the wedding. So much the better. He could study their sour faces at leisure when they came to call that very evening. He roused himself from his pleasurable thoughts.

"Morag."

"My lord?"

"My brither and his wife are to sup with us this evening. You are to wear your finest gown and you are to smile on me in a doting way . . . fetch me things and hang on the back of my chair. You are to tell the new Lady Fleming that I'm a powerful husband, understand?"

"Yes, my lord. It will be like a play, I think . . . although I have heard such things are sinful," she added thoughtfully.

"It seems tae me there's a great deal more sinful in that prudish mind of yours than play-going," said the earl looking at her curiously. "Have you never felt the passion of a woman for a man?"

Morag blushed painfully and stared at her plate.

"Is it something I should feel?" she countered at last.

"For God's sakes, what feel ye when I kiss ye?"

Morag wrinkled her pretty brow. The correct answer was "sick and suffocated" but she knew she should not say that.

"I d-do n-not know," she stammered. "I s-suppose my f-feelings are somewhat confused."

"Och, your mind's a mess," said the earl in disgust. "You're as cold as charity, Morag, and you'll always be the same. I would ha' expected it had I married that old hag, Simpson, but a young girl like yourself should have mair red bluid in her veins. But you're a fine-looking wench. I've a mind to try my leg over ye again. Let's to bed."

Morag's heart sank. She looked wildly toward the window where the countryside stretched out in an unobtainable vista of freedom. She had made her marriage vows and must obey, but she suddenly felt she could not bear the struggling weight of his old body again.

"I should spend the afternoon preparing for your brother's visit," she said hurriedly. "You would have me look my best."

The earl's sudden lust had fizzled and died. For all her great beauty, there was something repellently ladylike about Morag with her precise English, her straight back and her exquisite table manners. "Oh, very well," he grumbled. "Off with ye and leave me tae my wine."

Morag rose and curtsied and then hesitated in the doorway, suddenly timid.

"My lord."

"What?"

"Is there any chance we may visit Edinburgh one day?"

"I'm bound for Edinburgh tomorrow. You can come along provided ye behave yerself this evening."

"*Thank* you," cried Morag, rushing forward to plant an impulsive kiss on his cheek. She tripped lightly from the room.

"She's a child," grumbled the earl into his claret. "I cannae bed a child, and that one is never going to grow up. Never!"

Chapter Two

Murr Castle was only partly fortified, having been built in the middle of the sixteenth century in whinstone rubble with freestone facings. It was built on a small hill, a natural hollow at the east and southeast capable of being utilized for defense. It had a large round tower on each corner and a jumble of slate roofs and was surrounded by great walls some seventy yards from the castle which enclosed pleasant flower gardens and a lily pond. The ditch beyond the wall had been filled in long ago and the parkland and woods of the earl's estates stretched out beyond the walls all the miles to the winding silver twists and bends of the River Tay. The countryside looked rich and placid, unlike the wild and savage scenery of the Highlands to which Morag had been accustomed.

The drawing room in which the company met that evening was small and square and decked with trophies of the chase. Most of the first floor had originally consisted of a great banqueting hall but had since been divided into dining room, drawing room, morning room and saloon.

Stags' heads glared glassily down on the

guests. A large stuffed pike took up most of one wall and sailed silently through the gloom in the flickering shadow waves thrown up by the wavering candles. Two other walls were hung with dull green silk which moved and whispered in the scurrying draughts which scampered blithely through the rooms of the castle like so many lost children of the north wind. On the remaining wall, a great smoking fire crackled and spurted and sent a perfectly splendid blaze roaring right up the chimney so that the roof of the castle must have been very well heated indeed. None of the heat, however, seemed to permeate the drawing room, and if any additional chill were needed, it was amply supplied by Lord Arthur Fleming and his wife.

The couple managed to convey the impression that the earl was vulgar in the extreme and that his new bride was an ignorant schoolgirl. This they did without opening their mouths. Every time the earl spoke, they both gave infinitesimal shudders of disgust and Morag's timid social sallies were received with high-bred disdain.

Lord Arthur was a tall, thin man dressed in very fashionable, very tight clothes. His sparse hair was teased and combed into wispy artistic curls. He had flat, brown eyes and a rather rabbity mouth.

The Lady Phyllis was arrayed in fine India muslin. Her face was beautiful according to the current mode — she had a very small pursed mouth, large liquid brown eyes, a long straight

21

nose and a high forehead. Her cheeks had the strange, rigid, apple-red roundness of a wooden doll. Morag did not know that this was caused by rouge on the outside and wax pads on the inside. She had still an immense amount to learn about the uncomfortable vagaries of fashion.

Things were bad enough before supper, but no sooner were they seated at the table than the Earl of Murr began to make everything worse.

"Well, Arthur," he began. "It's sorry ye must be to see me married."

"Really! Why?" asked his brother coldly.

"Come, man, ye must have hoped to inherit. Aye — I'm sure ye didnae think for a minute that I would wed such a lusty young bride."

"Lusty, indeed," murmured Lady Phyllis coldly, making Morag feel as if her bosom were too large and her mouth too wide and her hair too red.

Lord Arthur dabbed fastidiously at his rabbity mouth with his napkin. "You are teasing, brother," he drawled in a high, fluting voice in which Scottish and English accents were perpetually at war. "I am well enough. Money is a vulgar subject and not fit for the dining table. Let us talk of something mair entertaining. We had a monstrous amusing time in London and had the honor to be invited to Lady Mumpers's ball."

"Did ye now?" said the earl with a great horse laugh. "Mumpers! Whita name. What was sae great about going there?"

22

"The Mumpers," said Lady Phyllis with a deprecating cough, "are related to the Fangles."

"Double Dutch to me," said the earl, swallowing claret in great noisy gulps.

Lady Phyllis gave a genteel sigh. "It is useless," she said, addressing her husband, "to talk of the *ton* in such surroundings. Ah, dear London. How I miss you!"

The earl picked up his gamecock from his plate and stuffed it in his mouth. "Issawunneryedonttayayre," he said.

"I beg your pardon," said his sister-in-law.

The earl spat out a small hail of crushed bones onto his plate. "I said, 'It's a wonder ye don't stay there' — or does it take too much siller?"

"We have money enough," remarked his brother.

"Oh, aye," sneered the earl, laying a finger alongside his nose. "Ye forget, I ken fine your lands are mortgaged to the hilt."

The earl returned to his chomping while a cold, hostile silence fell on the dining room. Morag racked her brains for something to say. At last she turned to Lady Phyllis, who was examining a piece of smoked lamb as if doubting the animal's pedigree. "You must tell me about the fashions of London, Lady Phyllis," she said, addressing that lady's cold face.

Phyllis looked down her long nose. "I think it would be a waste of time to try," she finally tittered. "High fashion is impossible to explain to the unsophisticated mind."

Morag's face flamed as red as her hair. "It seems to me," she replied in a level voice, "that being sophisticated means having no manners or breeding at all."

"Are you addressing me?" gasped Phyllis.

"Yes, I am . . . you whey-faced bitch," said Morag, gleefully using one of her husband's pet expressions. Morag was still very much a school-room miss.

The earl's great booming laughter seemed to fill the castle. "Go to it, Morag," he gasped when he could.

Lady Phyllis rose to her feet, her languid airs and poise melting away.

"How dare you, you common little strumpet!" she howled at Morag. "For the likes of you to criticize the likes of me. It makes me sick to . . . to . . ."

"Your stomach," said Morag helpfully, watching with fascination the cracking of Lady Phyllis's veneer.

With a great effort, Lady Phyllis pulled herself together. "Come, Arthur," she said grandly. "Take me away from this vulgar company."

Her lord looked down at the table. "Sit down," he said reluctantly. "You take things too much to heart. Don't refine on it so."

"We are leaving, d'ye hear," screamed Phyllis, leaning over the table and gazing at him as if she could not believe her eyes.

"Sit down!" squeaked her husband, "and dae as ye are told."

Phyllis collapsed in her chair, her eyes filling with shocked tears. Never before had her husband disobeyed her commands. Lady Phyllis could not know that her husband had just remembered the sole purpose of his visit — that of borrowing money from his rich brother — and that when he wished to borrow money, there was no one in the whole of Caledonia stern and wild who could be more single-minded.

And so she continued to sob over the tansey pudding and almost tottered when the time came to leave the gentlemen to their wine.

Morag followed her out, feeling miserable. It was one thing to be rude to the icy, haughty Lady Phyllis but another to be unkind to this pathetic weeping girl. Her soft heart was touched.

"I am truly sorry," said Morag awkwardly, "to have caused you such distress."

"Of *course* it was all your fault," said Phyllis, drying her eyes on a wisp of cambric and looking jealously at the younger girl's glowing beauty. "But you cannot blame me for saying you would not understand high fashion. Why — one has only to look at your gown."

"What is wrong with it?" asked Morag, curiosity overcoming her temper. She privately thought her gown of gold damask very fine.

"So outmodish," sighed Phyllis. "The cut is antique and one never wears such heavy materials. One has the waist of the gown *here*" — she pointed to below her bust — "and only wears the thinnest of muslins, even in winter."

"I am to go to Edinburgh tomorrow," ventured Morag. "Perhaps I may purchase something t-tonnish there." Morag stammered slightly over the pronunciation of the unaccustomed slang.

Phyllis treated her companion to a small, superior smile. "Edinburgh," she said in accents filled with loathing. Then she shrugged. "On second thought, perhaps *Edinburgh* will suit you very well."

"Why are you so rude and unkind?" Morag demanded hotly. "Because, really, you do it very badly."

Lady Phyllis looked totally nonplussed, but the door opened and the gentlemen entered. Both were in high spirits: Arthur because he had got his money, and the earl because he had had a most enjoyable time humiliating his younger brother — unaware that when it came to the pursuit of money, nothing could really humiliate Lord Arthur Fleming.

Arthur was so pleased with himself that he was inclined to flirt genteelly with Morag, a fact which distressed his wife even more.

Morag, for her part, could only be glad when the evening came to an end. Phyllis was the first young lady of nearly her own age she had met and the whole experience had been a sore disappointment.

There was more to follow. For after the unwelcome guests had gone, the earl cocked his great head on one side and listened to the song of the rising wind. "Weather's turning bad," he re-

26

marked. "We'll no be going to Edinburgh if this keeps up. Off tae bed with ye. I'm right proud of the way you told that puddin'-faced coo what you thought but, och, I've had enough of yer cauld manners."

Morag trailed miserably to her room. Nonetheless, she packed a trunk, listening all the while in case her husband should join her, dreading the prospect as she used to dread being dragged before her father for a beating. But the earl did not come. At last, she pulled the bed curtains close. She would never see Edinburgh, she thought unhappily. She would molder in this draughty castle until the day she died.

She awoke in the morning and lay very still. The sound of the wind had died and had been replaced by the sleepy chirping of birds. She drew back the bed curtains. A shaft of sunlight was shining through the small dusty window-panes into the room. A vision of Edinburgh rose before her eyes and she fairly scrambled into her clothes, tugging impatiently at tapes and buttons in her hurry to get dressed.

She was going after all!

The child that was Morag blithely skipped downstairs to take her leave of the castle — not knowing that she would return a woman.

Chapter Three

Morag prepared herself for a long task of persuading her incalculable husband to get ready, but when she descended the curved stone stairs, it was to find the earl not only ready but on the point of departure, his cumbersome traveling carriage having been brought round to the door.

He told her curtly that she would need to forgo breakfast if she wished to come and barely gave her time to don her bonnet and pelisse.

Morag sat on the edge of the carriage seat in an agony of anticipation, frightened the earl would change his mind. But the coachman cracked his whip, and, flanked by two outriders, the earl's carriage moved off.

It was barely seven in the morning and an early mist was burning off the fields. The sun flashed and jogged through the overhead trees on the castle drive and, as the carriage clattered out of the woods, out of the shelter of the trees, a flock of woodpigeons sailed up, swooping and diving under a sky of pale, washed blue.

Cow parsley spread their lacy heads through the red and thorny spikes of unripe brambles in the hedgerows and tangled vetch rioted in a mass of blue and purple. The clear air was like champagne. The carriage rolled sedately past a field of incredibly green grass which turned and rolled in the morning breeze like the waves of some enchanted ocean. The leaves were already turning to red and gold, and a hail of beechnuts rattled on the carriage roof. Now a field of stubble, blazing in the morning sun like cloth of gold, dotted with fat and roosting seagulls, looking awkward and strangely prehistoric so far from the sea.

Morag turned to say something to her husband but he had fallen asleep, his great head lolling to the swaying of the carriage and his wig askew. She felt a strong twinge of unease. She did not feel as if she had behaved like a proper wife. Her mind, still adolescent, still innocent, nonetheless told her that she should have welcomed her husband's attentions with more warmth. The castle housekeeper was efficient and the domestic arrangements of the castle were well run. Morag felt young and useless, a child adrift in an adult world.

Assailed by a feeling of loneliness so deep it was almost a physical pain, she longed to belong somewhere, anywhere. She missed her home. She even missed the severe and reproving face of Miss Simpson. Distance lent her stern father enchantment and imbued him with a parental kindliness he did not have.

She watched the passing fields through a mist of tears, all her excitement at seeing the capital gone.

Her distress was soon increased by sheer physical discomfort. The earl proved to be a good landlord for, as soon as the carriage had lurched from the boundaries of his land, the roads degenerated into little more than rutted tracks of dried mud, and more than once Morag's head came into contact with the carriage roof. The earl at last awoke after his own head had received what he termed "a sair dunt." The coach had at last to be abandoned for a pair of stout pack horses, and after two days of this form of travel, broken by nights in ill-kept inns, Morag began to feel an ache in her back and a blinding headache behind her eyes.

On the evening of the fourth day, they arrived in Edinburgh and made their weary way to the High Street.

The High Street ran from the Palace of Holyroodhouse along a ridge to the castle, a grim, medieval building which crouched atop a hundred-foot jumble of rocks. The mile-long street was bordered by gloomy tenements, built as far back as the sixteenth century.

Nothing had prepared Morag for the noxious smells emanating from these apartment houses which compressed between them a dark maze of sloping alleys and courtyards. There was ample evidence that this was the city where "every gentleman is a drunkard and every drunkard a gentleman." The apartments were often thirteen stories high and crammed with people; tailors, lawyers and aristocrats sharing the same building with a free and easy democracy which startled the English visitor.

The noise was incredible. Everyone seemed to be selling something at full pitch, although the light was fading — coals, white sand, herring — and the jumbled, jostling crowd was occasionally kept in order by the much-detested City-Guard, a band of fierce Highlanders who used battle-axes to keep the citizenry in line.

This then was Morag's first impression of the city of her dreams — noisy, smelly, gothic, medieval. But she was too tired to care.

She wearily followed the earl and his servants up a particularly vile-smelling close and then up a pitch-black narrow stone stair to the earl's apartments which were on the middle floors. To her relief, she was greeted by a motherly housemaid who was almost clean. The earl's "town house" was very small and dark, consisting only of five rooms and a kitchen. Morag had one bedroom; the earl, to her great relief, had the other. The three other rooms acted as parlor, dining room and drawing room. The housemaid bedded down under the dresser in the kitchen and the rest of the servants were put out for the night like so many household cats.

Morag arose early as usual, hearing the raucous clamor of the High Street rising faintly up on the cold, still air.

She climbed stiffly from her bed and moved to the window. The panes were so smeared with dirt that she thought what she saw through them

31

must be an optical illusion.

She opened the window and leaned out, gasping at first at the shock of the cold air and the fact that the ground plummeted down below her as if she were perched on the edge of a cliff.

Then she raised her eyes and there it was. Camelot! The Promised Land. The dream country.

Over the thousand-foot grimy span of the North Bridge which sprang out from the High Street lay another land. The elegant squares and houses of the New Town basked in the morning sun. The splendid terrace called Princes Street smiled benignly across smooth gardens and a great gully of jagged rock which cut it off from the squalor of the High Street.

Morag felt as if she were living in the Middle Ages seeing a vision of the future. There was an old brass bell on the washstand and she rang it loudly, waiting impatiently until the housemaid appeared, yawning, from the kitchen.

"What is that? Where is that?" cried Morag.

The maid peered sleepily out of the window. "Och, that's the New Town, my leddy. 'Tis where the gentry live now."

"Why don't we live there?" said Morag breathlessly.

"Oh, all the grand folk hivnae moved ower. The earl and some o' the ithers likes it fine here. 'Tis what they've been used to."

"What is it like?" cried Morag.

"It's a long way away, my leddy," said the maid

as if Morag had been asking her to describe America. "I hivnae had the time."

"I shall wake my husband directly and we will go there *now*," breathed Morag.

"My lord is oot and aboot," shrugged the maid, wiping her nose on the corner of her apron. "Gone tae see his cronies."

"I cannot go alone," said Morag desperately. "I know. *You* shall accompany me. What is your name?"

"Maggie — Maggie Sinclair," said the maid, remembering her manners and bobbing a curtsy. "I cannae go. I've a lot of work."

Morag bit her lip in vexation. "When will my husband return?"

"I cannae say. He aye goes to Dowie's Tavern for a dram and then tae the Right and Wrong Club and maybe on tae the Spendthrift."

"Then I shall go alone," decided Morag.

"I widnae dae that," said Maggie shaking her head. "Whit'll my lord say?"

My lord would not be in a fit state to say anything by the time he finished patronizing his favorite watering holes, thought Morag grimly, so she did not answer, merely proceeding to dress. Maggie shrugged and left. It was not for her to criticize her betters.

When Morag eventually ventured timidly out into the High Street, she shrank back from the jostling throng. But the New Town with its quiet gardens and squares beckoned so she pushed forward down the hill in the direction of the

North Bridge. She did not see the earl but he saw her. He had returned with some of his cronies to show them his beautiful, young wife, having already bragged a great deal about her charms.

But as he was about to hail her, his eye was caught by the sight of a servant girl bending over to lift a pail of water. Her ragged skirts were kilted up around a pair of well-turned, if dirty, ankles. A long rip in her skirt revealed tantalizing glimpses of pale leg.

The earl forgot about Morag, forgot about his friends. His hands twitched. "Deil tak' me," he muttered. "Will ye look at that!"

The girl turned around and caught the earl's avid stare. Bending down, she slowly raised her skirt. On her calf were the brave and tattered remains of a scarlet garter. Although it was obviously only doing service as an ornament, the lady having no stockings on, it seduced the earl's senses so much that he startled the street with a joyous "Halloo!" and bounded forward.

Morag hurried on, spurred by the sound of the wild cry behind her. She thought it sounded like a bull in pain.

Although several pawky gallants tried to block her path, she managed to avoid them and at last hurried over the North Bridge, her eyes fastened on the New Town beyond.

It was like stepping into another world. Edinburgh had already been established as the Athens of the North for some years and now boasted many English visitors who had come to see this peculiar city where society rated metaphysics higher than money.

Morag stared open-mouthed at the ladies in their thin dresses and wondered why they did not die of cold. She herself was wearing her blue wool dress with a pelisse buttoned over it and a shapeless bonnet. She turned to look after one young miss who was wearing so little that practically nothing was left to the imagination and, turning back, bumped full into a tall figure. She stammered her apologies and looked up into the greenest pair of eyes she had ever seen. They were not hazel with flecks of green nor were they that pale gooseberry color. They were as green as emeralds and as unwinking as the eyes of a cat. She ducked her head and muttered an apology and scurried off down Princes Street.

The sun shone down bravely and the air was warm until she came to one of the many crossings where an arctic wind whipped down all the way from the North Sea. A faint feeling of unease told her that she was being followed and she looked back. Sure enough, there he was — the man with the green eyes. The fleeting glimpse was enough to show her that he was tall and slim and very fashionably dressed. He wore a riding coat and buckskins, the little gold tassels on his glistening Hessian boots swung jauntily and the crisp white of his elaborate cravat, dazzling against the black of his jacket.

She turned round quickly as she caught the beginnings of a strange smile of . . . recognition?

. . . on his face. She felt strangely breathless and somehow obscurely threatened. She saw the cool dark doorway of a bookseller's shop and dived for cover, casting another quick look back.

Morag breathed a sigh of relief. He had been accosted by a party of friends. She found that the palms of her hands were damp and her knees trembling. What on earth was she afraid of?

She turned her attention to the bookshelves. So many, many books, hitherto forbidden. Miss Simpson was a great believer in the destructive influence of romantic literature. So although Morag was allowed to know the names of various famous writers, she had not been allowed to read their work.

She idly turned over the pages of a slim volume of poetry. It was secondhand and the pages had already been cut. "Poems," said the title page, "by the Reverend John Donne."

Feeling on safe and familiar ground, Morag began to read. Pandora's box was opened wide. Her eyes were fastened on the pages, her senses and emotions reeling under the impact of some of the most beautiful love poems in the world.

"All Kings, and all their favorites,
All glory of honors, beauties, wits,
The sun itself, which makes times, as they pass,
Is elder by a year, now, than it was
When thou and I first one another saw:
All other things, to their destruction draw,
Only our love hath no decay;

This, no tomorrow hath, nor yesterday,
Running, it never runs from us away,
But truly keeps his first, last, everlasting day."

She read on, her eyes misted with tears, feeling a strange lost yearning.

Her right to innocent love and passion had been forfeited by this arranged marriage to an old man. Her tremulous, adolescent half-formed feelings were being given a guide, an explanation, as she read her way steadily along the shelves, oblivious to the other customers and the dry, impatient cough of the bookseller.

Here was Shakespeare, there was Pope, all around her the witty, clever voices cried love. Andrew Marvell cynically berated his coy mistress. Was this how her husband felt?

"Then worms shall try
That long preserv'd virginity,
And your quaint honor turn to dust,
And into ashes all my lust,
The grave's a fine and private place,
But none, I think, do there embrace."

As the sun outside climbed higher in the sky over the grim castle, Morag read on, dazzled, moved, elated and despairing as she lost her emotional virginity in an orgy of reading.

The cough behind her was now sharp enough to make her swing around, blushing furiously.

The bookseller was a small, chubby man in a

pepper-and-salt frock coat and knee breeches. He had begun to assume that the young lady in the good but unfashionable clothes was under the misapprehension that she was in a circulating library and hoped to at least sell one book to her.

"Can I help you, madam?"

"Oh, yes. I mean, I would like to buy some books," said Morag, wildly scooping up armfuls. The bookseller's fat, white face creased up into a smile like that of a pleased baby. Then his face fell as his strange customer put the books down again and started scrabbling frantically in her diamond-shaped reticule.

"I have forgot to bring money," wailed Morag. She could not go home bookless; she could not!

The bookseller caught the gleam of gold on Morag's finger through the lace of her mittens. "Perhaps madam's husband . . . ?" he began.

"Yes, indeed," said Morag. "I shall find him and then I shall return. He is the Earl of Murr — perhaps you know our address. It is in the High Street and it should not take me very long to walk there and back . . ."

"That will not be necessary," said the bookseller with an avuncular smile. Oh, the magic of a title! "My lady may choose what she pleases and my boy, Jimmy, will carry them for you."

A half hour later, Morag set out for the High Street with Jimmy, the bookseller's boy, trotting behind her, bowed down under a sack of books — poetry, plays and, most priceless, several sets of novels which the bookseller had assured her were read by all the ladies of the *ton.*

For the next few days Morag did not leave the sanctuary of her room. She barely noticed her husband's absence, she barely noticed his return at the end of two days when he was helped up the stairs, having drunk himself into an inflammatory fever.

By systematically dosing himself with a mixture of brandy and mercury, the earl once again felt returned to the land of the living and remembered that his drinking friends had latterly begun to doubt the existence of this pretty wife he had bragged about so much.

He accordingly decided to promenade his wife down the High Street between the hours of one and two, which he vaguely remembered as the fashionable time to be seen. He brushed aside Morag's faltering apologies for the amount of books she had bought — although his lordship read little else other than the game laws and the *Guide to the Turf* — with the remark that the whole of Edinburgh was book daft.

Morag dressed in her finest clothes at his bidding and, her eyes still clouded with dreams, she allowed her husband to lead her into the jostling crowd on the High Street. The earl and his bride made their stately progress, only jumping nimbly away from the tenements as a wild cry of "Gardez loo" from above presaged the emptying of the contents of a chamberpot into the street.

The earl espied two of his elderly cronies and

hustled Morag forward. The men were called, it seemed, Erchie and Cosmo. They reeked of old spirits and their clothes were none too clean but they treated Morag with great admiration and courtesy, Erchie, who hailed from Glasgow, pronouncing her to be "a veritabubble ferry," which Morag translated into "veritable fairy" after some difficulty.

The courtesies being dealt with, the earl and his friends fell to comparing the virtues of various taverns. Soon the three were hard at it, gossiping, and each one plying that instrument which is euphemistically known as a back scratcher — an ivory hand at the end of a long stick — which is really for scratching at the livestock in your head without disturbing the hairdresser's art. Morag was left to survey the busy scene.

The day was steel-gray and cold. Edinburgh was giving a fine example of why it had earned its nickname, "Auld Reekie," as the fumes and smoke rising from the myriads of chimneys blotted out most of the little light from the lowering sky and turned midday into midnight. The crowd jostled and pushed, exchanging greetings, nobles and their ladies rubbing shoulders with the lowest of the citizens. Newhaven women with strident voices and striped aprons sold "caller herrin'," a knife grinder called his trade, his shrill voice rising above the other cries of pies and coal, soot and sand. Anyone who had anything to sell tried to sell it. An old man who seemed nothing more than a bundle of rags held together with string placed a dirty cloth on the ground and carefully placed on the cloth a pair of worn and cracked boots and proceeded to add his voice to the cacophony.

And then Morag experienced that strange feeling of unease. She turned her head slowly and across the jostling, moving throng, she met the gaze of a familiar pair of green eyes. Blue and green eyes met and held. Morag could not look away. For now she had poetry, wicked seductive poetry, to clarify her thoughts, and a quotation leapt unbidden into her head.

> "Our eye-beams twisted, and did thread
> Our eyes, upon one double string;
> So to entergraft our hands, as yet
> Was all the means to make us one,
> And pictures in our eyes to get
> Was all our propagation."

She blushed suddenly and painfully and dragged her eyes away.

"There she is again," murmured Lord Toby Freemantle.

"Where? Who?" demanded his friend, the Honorable Alistair Tillary.

"Toby means the redhead," drawled the third of the party, Harvey Wrexford. "Don't meddle with the local natives, Toby. You'll only come to harm."

The three Englishmen were visiting Edinburgh. Neither their fathers nor grandfathers would have been seen dead in the place, but Scotland was once again fashionable, and Edinburgh hailed as an intellectual paradise.

Lord Toby, of the green eyes, was twenty-five years old and had already earned himself a reputation as a rake. Part of it was well deserved but most was a fiction spread around by disappointed mothers of marriageable daughters. Lord Toby was an extremely wealthy young man. He was a model of athletic grace and exquisite tailoring. Life had been very easy for him and therefore had left him with a perpetual nagging feeling of boredom.

His two friends were equally fashionably dressed but neither was blessed with Lord Toby's romantic face and figure. Alistair Tillary was round and fat with a chubby, jovial face held prisoner by the enormously high starched points of his shirt. Harvey Wrexford was thin to the point of emaciation and had a long, mild face. He looked like an undernourished sheep.

"I must find out who she is," went on Lord Toby, his eyes fastening on a shining curl which had escaped from Morag's bonnet. "Did you ever see such hair?"

"It's red," yawned Alistair. "Very unfashionable."

"But such a red," said Toby. "It's almost purple, and, oh, those eyes! Who are these old men with her? One of them must be her father."

"All the more reason to leave her alone," said Harvey.

"Nonsense! She escaped me before. Look, there is a servant giving that one next to her a snuffbox. I shall catch him when he leaves and find out her name."

Lord Toby watched until the servant drew back a little into the crowd. Morag was staring at her boots. He approached the servant and dropped a couple of coins into the man's hand.

"You must refresh my memory," he said in a low voice. "What is the name of your master?"

The servant was Highland and had no love of the English but he had accepted the money and his rigid code of honor told him he would need to give this accursed Sassenach the information he wanted. "Earl of Murr," he mumbled in a surly voice and melted away into the crowd.

Lord Toby stared at the back of Morag's head and felt his heart begin to beat quickly. He was not in love, of course. He was too hardheaded a young man to think that anyone fell in love at first sight — that is, if anyone actually ever fell in love at all. He gave a deprecatory cough and said, "Lord Murr?"

"Whit issit? Whit issit?" grumbled the earl, cross at having his gossip interrupted.

"May I introduce myself," pursued Lord Toby. "My name's Freemantle, fifth viscount of the name."

"Oh, aye," grunted the earl. "An Englishman, I've nae doot. Well, whit dae ye want, laddie?"

Lord Toby fought down a mad impulse to say, "I want *her*," but instead hit on a brilliant idea. "I have heard you praised as having the finest palate in Scotland for claret," he said. "I wonder if it could possibly match my own since I am accounted something of an expert in the south. I would be prepared to supply several pipes of your favorite vintage if you would care to meet me to sample some vintages I have lately acquired."

Lord Toby tried to catch Morag's eye again but she was still looking down.

The earl studied him cautiously. For all his family's politics and religion, old loyalties die hard and he did not particularly want to drink with an Englishman, but his two cronies were enthusiastic. "I'd take his lordship's kind offer masell," said Cosmo.

"Aye, you *would*," sneered the earl. "You'd drink wi' the deil hisself if it got you a free drink. Och, very well, laddie. Gie us your direction."

Lord Toby produced his card and handed it over. "Will eight o'clock this evening be suitable?" he asked, thinking all the while, "Will she never look up?"

"Eight o'clock will be just fine," said the earl.

Lord Toby hesitated. "I do hope your charming daughter will not be angry with me for taking you away this evening."

"Daughter?" said the earl and then let out a great bellow of laughter. "This is my wife, laddie."

Lord Toby felt an almost physical stab of pain in the region of his heart. This beautiful girl wed to this old satyr. Morag had taken the earl's arm and the earl pressed his wife's hand and then released it to fiddle about his wig with the back scratcher.

Morag's burst of loyalty to her husband could not stop her from looking up at Lord Toby, at those fascinating green eyes, at the strong, handsome face, at the humorous, sensuous mouth.

Lord Toby caught his breath. There was such bewilderment and pain in the girl's eyes that he quickly averted his own. These waters were too deep for him. But he would still have to endure the earl's company.

He bowed and returned to his friends. Some innate kindness stopped him from telling them that Morag was the earl's wife. He merely said curtly that the girl was affianced and, turning on his heel, thrust his way through the crowd, leaving his friends to follow.

The day grew blacker and a fine drizzle began to fall. Lord Toby shook his head slightly to try to dispel the picture of the beautiful girl, blazing like a jewel in the squalor of the High Street. He had always prided himself on being a practical, level-headed man who enjoyed his various amours with just the right degree of cynicism. Damn this weird, smoky capital with its medieval buildings. It caused disturbing fancies in the mind.

Evening fell on Edinburgh, on rich and poor alike. On Morag, sitting crying over her books in one room, on the earl being lashed into his corsets in the other.

Reading would not allow Morag to escape anymore. Every hero had green eyes and jet black hair.

The earl had once asked her if she had ever felt the passion of a woman for a man.

"Oh, indeed I have, my lord. Indeed I have!" cried Morag to the silent walls as the earl clattered down the stairs, a romantic figure to Morag for the first and only time, because he was going to see Lord Toby.

Chapter Four

Winter settled its steely grip on the land, on Perthshire and on Murr Castle.

On his return from Edinburgh, the earl had had all the chimneys swept with the result that the fires no longer smoked but all the heat went up to the roof more than ever and kept the innumerable birds nesting cozily in the turrets from freezing.

The days stretched out long and gray and silent. Morag's one excitement was the arrival of the carrier from Perth with another consignment of books. As the long days passed, the heroes between the pages began to take on their own given coloring and identity. The knights and lords and poets no longer had black hair and green eyes. But memory remained and Morag found it increasingly hard to accept the fact that she was tied for life to this loveless marriage and her virgin state.

There were, however, some things to be thankful for. The earl no longer seemed to want to bed his wife. Rapidly failing health and a preoccupation with the scullery maid kept him fully occupied. Sometimes in the dark evenings, he would ask Morag to read to him, enjoying the simpler stories with an almost childlike absorption. Gradually a strange kind of affection grew between the earl and his young wife. Like a small child, he would look forward to his "bedtime story," his gouty foot propped up on a footstool, watching the light of the flames play in Morag's red hair and listening with pleasure to the clear, soft notes of her voice. A little of the old, soft Scottish burr of childhood had crept back into Morag's voice, a little of the Highland lilt.

Sometimes the earl would rouse himself to tell her again of that strange evening in Edinburgh with Lord Toby Freemantle since she never seemed to be tired of hearing it. Of how the young lord had indeed had a good palate for wines. He fortunately did not tell Morag that as the wine had sunk lower in the bottles, he had regaled his young lordship with some very warm and fictitious stories of Morag's amorous expertise.

He praised instead Lord Toby's meticulous courtesy and wondered again why this English stranger had gone to such trouble to entertain a man old enough to be his father, a man he had only met that day.

Then the earl would add, "Aye, a fine lad for an Englishman. Hell-bent on emulating Boswell and Johnson. I told him he was welcome here but, och, although it hasnae snowed I doubt if he's coming." And Morag would experience that terrible pang of half hope, half despair.

The winter skies grew heavier and darker and the wind no longer blew from the North Sea but swung round to the west bringing with it that damp, almost metallic smell, the harbinger of snow.

First it came in infinitesimal white specks, so light, they barely settled on the ground. Then they grew larger until Morag, looking out of the castle window, could see great sheets of white blowing across the countryside, first blotting out the silver wind of the river, then the fields, then the castle gardens.

Suddenly the clouds parted and a single shaft of sunlight shone down, turning the land to blinding white, highlighting the massive purple snowclouds, lighting up a small figure in the distance, a figure on horseback, riding toward the castle.

Morag felt a pang of anticipation, fear, elation. Could the solitary horseman be Lord Toby? Then the heavy clouds blotted out the sun and the snow fell harder than ever and the small figure was lost to view.

It could not be he, of course. He would come with his friends. Or, failing that, he would have a manservant riding behind him and a pack pony for his baggage. An hour passed and no halloo came from the castle courtyard.

Well, at least the foul weather would keep Lord Arthur and Lady Phyllis away. Their visits had become quite frequent. Morag did not know why, because they obviously detested the earl and Lady Phyllis's sole amusement seemed to be in deriding Morag's face, figure and clothes.

A three-volume novel lay beside her with its pages as yet uncut. Morag was frightened to start reading it in case she finished it too quickly. There would be no more books from the book-seller until winter slackened its grip.

She froze as the muffled sound of voices came up to the window and the stamping of hooves and the whickering of a horse.

Morag sat as if turned to stone. She heard one of her husband's servants mounting the stairs to the earl's bedchamber. After some time, she heard his slow, shuffling steps on the stairs and his voice saying, "Lord Toby Freemantle, d'ye say? Well, well, well. It'll be grand to have a bit of company."

Then his voice, raised in welcome, resounded from below and the sound of his great laugh. "I must keep my dreams," thought Morag wildly and illogically. "He is only a very ordinary young man after all." But as two sets of footsteps could be heard mounting the stair, she scampered wildly from the room and escaped to the safety of her bedchamber. She rang the bell.

It was eventually answered by Fionna Ingles, the earl's scullery maid, who had been elected to the grand position of housemaid, despite the housekeeper's patent dislike of the girl and her complaints that Fionna Ingles was "nothing mair than a sleekit quean."

Fionna seemed to have grown considerably

fatter than Morag had remembered. She had heard whispers that her husband took his pleasures in the servants' quarters and wondered for the first time whether Fionna's were the quarters that he took them in.

"My leddy rang," pointed out Fionna sulkily, smoothing her apron down over her large stomach.

"Tell my lord I am indisposed," said Morag. "I will join him at supper."

Then perhaps Lord Toby will have left, thought poor Morag, but the howl of the rising storm seemed to mock that hope.

Fionna shuffled out, casting a jealous eye on the new gown Morag had been making which was spread over a chair.

Morag spent the rest of the day in a fever of fear and anticipation. She wanted him to leave and at the same time dreaded his going. She stitched diligently to finish her new gown, vowing one minute that it didn't matter in the slightest what she looked like and the next, hoping he would find her as fashionable as the young ladies of London. Morag had found time between book buying in Edinburgh to purchase several yards of sprigged India muslin. Now she was fashioning it into the latest style — high waist, little puff sleeves, low neckline and a deep flounce at the hem.

Although the earl had his valet, Morag did not have a lady's maid so there was no one to tell her whether her appearance in the new gown was suitable to that of a young Scottish countess.

Lord Toby watched her entering the room. He could have told her volumes.

He had not forgotten her. It was like a sickness, he decided. He had ridden as far as Perth with his two companions, who had refused to go any farther. Toby's plan to ride out and visit the Earl of Murr for a few hours was considered madness. Alistair had pointed out that if they did not quickly start for the south, then they would be stranded in this accursed country until the spring.

Lord Toby had set out alone, promising to return in time for supper. And as if in mocking answer to Alistair's prophecy, the snow began to fall heavily.

He felt he ought to turn back. On the other hand he was more determined to exorcise the vision of Morag from his brain.

His welcome at the castle had been reassuring in a way. It all seemed very primitive. The earl seemed older and more bloated than he had remembered.

And then she walked into the room, the thin muslin floating about her body, her neck, rising from the dainty neckline looking like alabaster and her hair, burning in the shadowed light.

He bent over her hand, apologizing for his riding dress. He had not known he would be stranded, he said in his light pleasant voice. She must forgive him. And Morag clutched onto his hand and felt the solid stone floor of the castle melt beneath her feet.

"You look braw," said the earl gruffly. "I wish that long-nosed caillich, Phyllis, could see ye noo."

The warmth and admiration in the earl's face made Toby's heart sink. He remembered the earl's description of Morag's talents which he had then only half believed but which now all seemed possible. But he could not take his eyes off her.

Left to the young couple, supper would have been an embarrassed, silent affair but the earl was in full flight, stuffing food in his mouth and laughing through it at his own jokes, spraying the table with bones and crumbs.

Morag passed a heavy wooden trencher to Lord Toby and their hands accidentally met and she snatched hers away as if they had been burned.

"I am behaving like the veriest moonstruck youth," thought Toby savagely. He roused himself to entertain his host with the gossip from Edinburgh. He had a lively wit and the earl seemed at times in danger of having an apoplexy, he laughed so hard.

The earl capped Lord Toby's stories with some of his own. They were decidedly warm anecdotes to relate in the presence of a lady but very funny for all that, and Toby found himself reluctantly warming to his Falstaffian host.

When they were seated by the fire in the drawing room, the earl suddenly begged Morag to read to him with a half-apologetic smile in the direction of Lord Toby. "I like a guid story," he smiled, "and Morag reads them that well."

Morag flushed and began to read, stumbling over the words at first until, with a Herculean effort, she shut Lord Toby's presence from her mind and concentrated on the narrative. The book was *Roderick Random* by Tobias Smollett, a writer very much after the earl's heart, and a choice of literature which would have shocked governess Miss Simpson's heart to the core. "He was formed for the ruin of our sex," read Morag in her pretty, soft voice while the earl chuckled appreciatively and Toby sat with his senses reeling, free to stare at Morag as much as he liked.

She read until the embers glowed red in the fire. She read until a gentle snore from the earl told her that her husband had fallen asleep.

She stopped reading and sat very still. Then she slowly raised her eyes and looked at Lord Toby.

Their eyes met and held. Morag felt a heavy, lethargic sweetness in her body.

Almost frightened of her, he rose to his feet. "It is late, madam," he said in a strained voice which did not sound like his own.

Morag rose too and dropped him a curtsy and then, as if impelled by some force greater than the social laws, she put her hand on the rough sleeve of his riding jacket.

He covered it with his own and stood looking

down at her, so close that he could feel the warmth from her body, feel the faint trembling of the hand under his own.

Then the earl stirred in his sleep and yawned. Morag snatched her hand away and with a breathless "Good night" fled from the room to the privacy of her bedchamber, to sleep with the hand he had held, cradled against her cheek.

The earl was roused by his servant and helped off to bed. Lord Toby found his own bedchamber, painfully aware of the proximity of Morag in this small castle.

He tossed and turned between the cold, damp sheets in the cold, damp room and struggled with his conscience. But the call of nature can take precedence even in the most anguished soul and he realized he would need to investigate the plumbing of the castle which, if he remembered rightly, consisted of a garderobe in the east tower, the hygienic arrangements of the castle not having been changed since the Middle Ages.

He was returning to his room when he heard the sound of a stifled female giggle coming from the earl's room. All his dreams fled faced with this cold reality. The countess was, of course, in bed with the earl and having a high old time by the sound of it. Toby cursed himself for a romantic fool and was about to take himself off to bed when the door of the earl's bedchamber opened. He did not want to meet her. He shrank back into the shadows.

The door swung wider. In the dim gold light of

the oil lamp by the earl's bedside stood a female figure which Lord Toby recognized as the housemaid, Fionna. She was scantily dressed. The earl followed her to the door and clutched her to him in a passionate embrace while Toby's heartbeats quickened with disgust and a strange hope. The goddess of his dreams was sleeping alone while her husband philandered with the maid — was in love with the maid, for there could be no doubting that expression on the earl's bloated face.

Toby waited until Fionna, with one last flirtatious wave of her hand to the earl, had pattered past him to her own quarters.

Then he went to his own room, impatient for the morrow, troubled by a fevered conscience — for she was married after all, and seemingly fond of her husband.

The next day dawned cold and gray but at least the snow had ceased. But again she did not appear and again the message was that her ladyship would be present at supper. He had to content himself until then.

The earl stayed in his rooms as well and there was little he could find to do apart from reading and eating. What kind of life was this for a young girl like Morag? he thought fretfully. The snow was lying deep and crisp and even under a leaden sky which promised more to come. I would die of boredom an I lived here, thought Lord Toby, suddenly homesick for the lights and color of London.

He was then confined to *his* room for two impatient hours before dinner while his shirt was laundered and his jacket brushed. He thought of the excellent wardrobe he had left behind with his friends in Perth.

At last it was time to dress and descend to the drawing room. His heart beating hard, he pushed open the door.

No one.

He paced up and down.

At last the door swung open and Morag stood timidly on the threshold. She was wearing a green silk gown of old-fashioned cut. It emphasized the tininess of her waist and the whiteness of her shoulders. Her red hair was piled on top of her head allowing one stray curl to lie on her shoulder.

As they stared at each other, tongue-tied, Fionna appeared behind Morag, bobbing a curtsy. The earl, she said, was sore plagued with the toothache and was keeping to his bed.

Lord Toby took a deep breath. He must remember to behave like a gentleman. He must remember, at all times, that this beautiful girl was married to his host.

He kept up an amiable if stilted conversation until they were seated at dinner and the servants had retired, the earl believing in the old-fashioned idea that one served oneself.

Morag had replied to all his conversational sallies with "yes" and "no" and "really," her eyes all the time fixed on her plate.

Wine loosened Toby's tongue, and despite his better nature, he at last could not help asking, "How did you come to meet your husband?"

"My father introduced us," said Morag, her eyes flying upward to meet his.

"He is somewhat older than you," pursued Toby gently. "Forgive me if I seem overfamiliar, Lady Murr, but I cannot help thinking you lead a very dull life. Have you no visitors?"

"Oh, yes," said Morag. "My lord's brother, Lord Arthur Fleming, and his wife, Lady Phyllis, come to call."

He refilled her glass. "Ah, that is then company for you. Is Lady Phyllis of your age?"

Morag drained her glass nervously in one gulp.

"No," she said. "I mean, yes, she is of my age."

"No? Do you not like her?"

"I would like her well enough," said Morag, feeling suddenly lighthearted with the effects of the wine, "but she does not like me. She criticizes my face and dress whenever we meet."

"You are very beautiful," said Toby, ignoring the warning bells in his head. "Many women would be jealous of you."

"You are kind, sir," replied Morag. "But that is not the case with Lady Phyllis." She gave a little laugh. "She is a soor-faced coo."

"I beg your pardon."

"Oh, I must translate for you. That is what my husband calls her — it means a sour-faced cow. She is in fact very beautiful and her cheeks are very round — like a doll's."

"That fashion is leaving us slowly," smiled Lord Toby. "Not many women wear wax pads in their cheeks nowadays."

"Wax pads!" said Morag, unconsciously putting her elbows on the table and savoring her first gossip. "Are there many such artifices?"

"Very many. False everything, I think," said Toby, remembering a disastrous affair with a dashing widow who had removed everything before bed leaving little left but a rag, a bone and a hank of hair. Morag thought of the earl and his corsets and false calves and false hair and giggled.

"You must tell me the joke," he teased her.

"I cannot," said Morag with an adorable blush.

"You are not thinking of yourself," he cried in mock horror. "Do not tell me those charms I see before me are unreal!"

"No, no," cried Morag, a little tipsily. They were seated quite close together at the small dining table. She leaned toward him, holding out that tantalizing lock of hair. "See, it is all my own."

He twirled the silken lock round one long finger. Something was happening to his breathing. He had drunk too much, too quickly. He abruptly threw caution to the winds.

"Ah, that I had the right to take inventory of the rest," he said, holding her blue eyes trapped in his green gaze.

Morag put out her hand to extract the lock of

hair from his. He caught her hand and, turning it over, pressed a burning kiss against her wrist.

"I should leave," he said quietly. "You fascinate me . . . Morag."

Morag thought of the days to come, the blank, long empty, loveless days stretching out to the grave.

"Don't go," she said in a whisper.

He rose to his feet and pulled her to hers. He drew her slowly to him and folded his arms about her and she laid her head against the rough sleeve of his jacket. Her body seemed to be on fire. She was trembling. They were both trembling.

He raised her chin and bent his mouth to hers, moving his lips against her own, pressing closer and deeper while Murr Castle whirled around and around and disappeared, leaving them stranded and alone on an empty plain of passion.

It was fortunate for both their reputations that the servant carrying in the pudding was clumsy. He fumbled and rattled at the door before he succeeded in getting it open. By the time he entered, both were at their places at the table, breathing heavily.

"Och, yis havnae touched a bite," said the servant, Hamish, with true Scottish democracy. "Well, naithin's lost what a pig'll eat. That'll go right fine in the servants' hall. Was yis wantin' puddin'?"

Both shook their heads. "We will retire to the drawing room," said Lord Toby, finding his voice. He rose and held out his arm. Hamish looked quickly at them both and clattered the dishes energetically. He was a large hairy Highlander who had been in the earl's service for the past ten years.

Lord Toby's one thought was to slam and lock the door of the drawing room and take Morag in his arms. Morag's one thought was to let him do just that. Hamish's new-sprung thought was to stop the couple doing anything at all.

To Lord Toby's amazement, Hamish shouldered his way after them into the drawing room. "Whit a puir wee bit of a fire," he said cheerfully. "I'll hae that fixed in a trice."

But he took a painfully long time about it, raking out the ash, placing logs on one by one.

Lord Toby drew Morag aside. "I shall come to your room later. I must see you. We cannot talk with this fellow here. Please wait for me," he whispered, and dizzy with love and wine, Morag nodded.

Lord Toby then loudly and clearly said he was going to make an early night of it and tried not to be irritated at the relief on the servant's face.

He held the door open for Morag, whispering very quietly as she passed him, "Later. Much later. When all are abed."

Morag paced her room for the next hour. What on earth was she doing? Was it so wrong to snatch just one little bit of happiness?

And then she heard the earl cry out, "Morag!" in a great wail of anguish. She hurried to his room.

He was propped up against the pillows, his face swollen and feverish.

"Oh, Morag, Morag!" he cried. "I cannae thole the pain o' this tooth any longer. I've been trying tae howk it out masell but I cannae."

"Perhaps one of the servants . . ." began Morag, moving close to the bed.

"Not them. I'm a coward when it come tae my teeth and it disnae do tae let the servants see it. Ye'll need tae do it for me, Morag."

He waved a small silver pair of pincers at her.

"I can't," said Morag, backing away.

"Come along, lassie. I'll die o' the pain." Morag thought of Lord Toby. Even now he might be approaching her room. She owed the earl something — even if it was only pulling a tooth.

She approached the bed again and leaned over him. "Very well," she said, taking up the pincers. "Which one?"

"Is un," said the earl, opening his mouth wide and pointing feverishly. Morag stared into the pit of decay in dismay. Which one of all these rotting teeth did he mean?

"Is un," gabbled the earl again, laying his finger on a crumbling tombstone at the front.

Morag knelt on the bed beside him and cautiously put the pincers round the aching tooth. The earl braced himself against the pillows. Morag shut her eyes and pulled and pulled and pulled. Finally she gave one tremendous wrench and somersaulted back onto the floor with the pincers, holding the decayed tooth clutched triumphantly in one hand.

The earl gave a great groan of relief. "Och, Morag, my love, my precious," he cried. "Naebody could ha' done that like you." And Morag laughed with pleasure at being able to help him.

Lord Toby had gone to Morag's room and had found it empty. He stood in the corridor, frowning. She couldn't be in her husband's room. Could she?

And then he heard the noises from the earl's room. Drawn by some awful fascination, he moved slowly forward and listened. He heard the creaking of the bed, the grunts of exertion and the earl's wild groans culminating in a great shout of relief. Then he heard the earl's shout, "Och, Morag, my love, my precious. Naebody could ha' done that like you." And then he heard Morag's laugh.

Lord Toby felt the bile rising in his throat. Strumpet! Morag was no innocent but a devilish woman who could drive him to the point of madness and then bed with her aged husband — that obscene bag of wind — as if nothing had happened. He remembered the earl's bawdy praise of his wife in Edinburgh and felt sick to his soul.

In vain did Morag wait out the rest of the night. As a livid dawn rose over the snow-clad landscape, she fell into an exhausted sleep.

She awoke late and to new hope. Of course, he had not come to her bedchamber. He was a gentleman, after all. She loved him the more for it. But today was a new day and she would see him again.

Despite the freezing chill of the castle and an itching in her toes which presaged chilblains, she dressed herself in her new muslin gown and ran lightly down the stairs.

The rooms were cold, stale and deserted. Hamish was hunched over the drawing room fire as if he had been there all night.

"Good day, my leddy," he said, turning round. "That young lord has left. Now I told him, I told him straight, he'd be as dead as a doornail before he ever saw Perth — riding out in this weather. Och, the English are all mad."

"Did he leave a message?" asked Morag faintly.

"Yes, a wee note. I have it here. It's for my lord."

Morag tore open the letter, her eyes darting along the few lines.

Nothing. Nothing for her. Only a chilly, formal note thanking the earl for his hospitality.

Gone.

She fumed and ran from the room, ran to the top of the castle, scarcely feeling the bite of the icy wind cutting through the thin muslin of her dress as she balanced on the leads and gazed frantically over the countryside.

There was a little black dot moving slowly in the distance.

"Toby!" she screamed. "Toby! T . . . o . . . b . . . y!"

But the black dot became a speck and then was swallowed up in the cold, staring whiteness of the landscape.

"Toby," she sobbed, clutching the stone battlements and feeling her heart break.

There was a shuffling, lumbering, wheezing step on the tower stairs and then the earl was beside her. He gently prised her fingers from the battlements, mopping at her tear-streaked face with the tail of his coat, muttering half-forgotten phrases, the kind you use to a hurt child.

"There, there. You come with me. We'll get cozy over the teacups and we'll forget about the whole thing. I could see what was in the wind. But we'll say nae mair. Come, come. Come with old Roderick. Roderick'll tak' care of ye."

"Yes, Roderick," said Morag brokenly, clinging to him. And even in the depths of her misery, she realized that she had never spoken the earl's Christian name until that moment.

Chapter Five

By the end of another month, Lord Toby was nothing more than a dragging, shameful ache in Morag's heart. She had nearly broken her marriage vows and all because of some callow, philandering, English buck who had led her on. No doubt in the clear light of dawn he had been thoroughly shocked at her wanton behavior. She could only, bitterly, hope he was shocked at his own.

God was issuing just punishment, thought Morag, the only God she knew being a Calvinistic one, incapable of charity or mercy and delighting in visiting terrible punishments on the sinner.

She felt debased. Her books were left unopened. Miss Simpson had been right. Treacherous literature had seduced her mind and tempted her from the proper path.

She thought the earl had regretted his forgiving kindness to her because he seemed to be sunk in gloomy meditation most of the time, occasionally throwing her furtive, sly looks from under lowering brows.

A brief thaw made the roads passable again bringing Lord Arthur and Lady Phyllis. Lord

Arthur had no need of money that day and so was on his worst behavior, managing to get under his brother's thick hide. Lady Phyllis simpered and tittered and derided and was particularly spiteful to the earl's housekeeper, Mrs. Tallant. Now although the earl at times cursed and berated his servants, he was very fond of them, and Lady Phyllis's treatment of his housekeeper riled him so badly that Morag feared he might have a seizure.

After the unwelcome couple had left and Morag was about to retire for the night, the earl begged her to stay with him. He had something serious to talk about.

"Come and sit by me, Morag," he said, indicating the footstool at his feet. He waited until she was settled and then, stroking her glistening hair with his heavy hand, began to speak.

"Fionna's with child. And it's mine. No, stay. Hear me out. I love the girl but, auld rip that I am, I at least know what's due tae my name. I cannae marry her. Quietly, now. Don't look sae shocked. I've fathered mair bastards than you've had hot meat. She'll no' suffer. I'll marry her off. But that brither o' mine. I've never cared much, Morag, about him inheriting but I care now. Deil tak' him! He's a bad landlord and a bad master and you'd not see a penny, Morag.

"So, I'm asking ye a favor, lassie. I want ye tae claim the child as your own."

"It's impossible," cried Morag. "Everyone would know."

"Listen, wheesht. Only Mrs. Tallant'll know apart from Fionna herself and she disnae want the babe. Ye could pad yer gowns and we could tell the world you are expecting an heir. That way everbody's future would be safe."

"But how . . . ?"

"Haud yer wheesht. Listen! When the bairn's near due, we leave for Edinburgh, you, me, Fionna and Mrs. Tallant. Mrs. Tallant has a' the skill o' a midwife. Fionna stays in Edinburgh. We return wi' the babe."

Morag twisted full round and looked up into his face. "It is a great deal to ask of me," she cried.

"Oh, aye?" said the earl dryly. "And if thon birkie, Freemantle, had had his way . . . aye, what then? Ye expect a lot frae me, Morag. Give a little!"

Morag's already sore conscience was struck another blow. She had not been a good wife. She did not know that her husband's appetites could only be roused by the lower class and had long assumed his lack of success with her was because of her own lack of love. The least she could do was provide him with an heir — albeit by proxy.

She rose and walked to the window, staring out at the wild black night. Somewhere out there were wives and husbands, ordinary families who lived their placid, respectable lives unplagued by bastards or passion. "Sorry for yourself?" sneered her ever active conscience. "You got off lightly."

"Very well," she said, swinging round. "I will do it."

"Good lass," said the earl. "We'll see my man o' business in Edinburgh at the same time and turn the whole thing ower tae him. I hae a lot of property and a fine house in London, too. I'll see Arthur well enough but you'll have the rest in keeping for the bairn until he's twenty-one. I'll appoint a steward tae look after the lands so ye won't be bothered wi' the managing o' the estates. I ken a fine fellow . . ."

"You sound as if you don't expect to live long," said Morag as lightly as she could.

"I don't think I will," said the earl seriously. "My guts are fair rotted. Aye, we've made a sorry mess o' things, Morag. Now, then, ye havnae read me anything in a while. What aboot a wee story. I like that cheil Roderick Random fine — me being Roderick as well."

He settled back in his chair with a smile of anticipation as Morag went to fetch the volume. Morag envied him his detachment. He had dealt with the problem and forgotten it already.

Morag read on, her mind busy with preparations. Women no longer wore pads, a fashion of years before where a pad of horse hair was worn under the front of the dress to simulate a look of pregnancy, but the shops of Perth were old-fashioned enough and would surely still have some in stock.

She broke off the narrative and looked up. "Do you never use the house in London, Roderick?"

"Eh, what's that? No, not these many years. I let it out for the Season, ye ken. It's in Albemarle Street. I havnae seen it this twenty year."

Morag wrenched her sinful mind away from thoughts of traveling to London, living in the house, and inviting over that treacherous, fickle Lord Toby. It was madness. He would never hurt her again. She would never see him again.

Winter reluctantly gave way to a chilly spring. Morag placed increasingly larger pads under her gowns and accepted the frigid compliments of Lady Phyllis, who quite patently hoped that this usurper would be stillborn.

At last, the savage gales and driving wind left the countryside smiling under a pale sun. When the first leaves were springing out from the skeletal branches, Morag, the earl, Fionna and Mrs. Tallant took the road to Edinburgh. Hamish had been let into the plot, the earl, whose health had been rapidly worsening, needing at least one man to help him on the journey.

The roads were still bad and they had to move at a snail's pace on horseback because of Fionna's delicate condition. They were still a good way from Edinburgh when Fionna's pains began.

"Bear up," said the earl. "We're only a mile from old Cosmo's place. Bear up, Fionna." Morag remembered Cosmo, Laird of Glenaquer, as one of the men in the High Street when Lord Toby had introduced himself to the earl.

"It's nae use," said Mrs. Tallant grimly. "Some things'll no wait."

And so it was that the future tenth Earl of Murr was born in a field under a smiling spring sky, a drift of hawthorn blossom blowing across his face and causing Mrs. Tallant to cry to heaven for forgiveness. "It's the fairy flower," she moaned. "The wean is cursed."

Ever practical, the earl slapped her hysterics quiet and sent Hamish off to his friend Cosmo with a frantic message, begging for a carriage, a wet nurse, and a body of strong men. Fionna lay white and exhausted, her face the color of the drifting hawthorn blossom. Morag held the squalling, raging, hungry baby against her useless breasts and prayed blindly and savagely for help, tears pouring down her face.

But by the time Cosmo arrived at the head of a body of men and with a traveling carriage bearing a wet nurse, Fionna was dead, all traces of her ordeal having been washed away by the efficient Mrs. Tallant. Great sobs racked the earl's body as Cosmo closed Fionna's eyes and gruffly ordered the servants out of earshot. The wet nurse took the baby away to the comfort of the carriage and Morag wrapped her arms round her husband, trying to find words of comfort.

Finally a sad procession made their way toward Cosmo, Laird of Glenaquer's home. Morag now felt drained of all emotion and unutterably weary. She dimly realized with some surprise that Cosmo's home was modern and comfortable but she soon tumbled headlong into sleep.

When she awoke, it was to find the wet nurse standing beside her bed, the baby in her arms. "Here he is, my leddy," said the nurse proudly. "A fine wee man. Lucky it is I had the milk, my ain having just died. Ah, well, I've five healthy ones and that's enough."

She placed the sleeping baby in Morag's arms and Morag looked down wonderingly at the small face, feeling a strong sense of maternal love.

"What is your name?" she asked the nurse at last.

"Helen MacDonald, my leddy. My husband's in service as footman to the laird."

"Leave him with me, Helen," said Morag, "but tell my lord I will join him shortly."

"Och, my leddy. It's havers you're talking. You'll no be gettin' up for a while."

Morag blinked and then remembered she was supposed to have given birth to this child.

"It was a shame about that lassie," went on Helen. "To fall deid just when you were having your baby and needed all the help you could get."

"Indeed, yes." Poor Fionna. "But I feel very strong," said Morag.

Helen did not answer but went out shaking her head. That was the Quality for you. Tough as old boots. "Just had a bairn and there she was, standing on the grass as neat as a new pin," Helen told the other servants. "The lass that died looked mair as if she had given birth than my leddy."

Morag lay back against the pillows, cradling the baby. Now Cosmo was in the secret as well. So many people to be bound to secrecy!

But this baby would be as much hers as if she had given it birth. That way she could make amends for her sinful love for Lord Toby; for the earl's adulterous affair with Fionna. The child would not suffer.

"I shall call you Roderick," she said softly to the sleeping child. Perhaps this child would compensate the earl for his lost love. He must be suffering terribly.

The large figure of the earl wandered aimlessly around his friend Cosmo's estate during the following week. He did not drink, he ate little, he showed no intcrest in the child apart from saying dryly that "it was a good thing it wasn't a girl or he would have gone through the whole posher for nothing," a comment which caused the servants to shake their heads and say the earl was a hard man.

He felt too weary to continue the journey to Edinburgh and sent for his man of business, lawyer James Murray, to come to him instead. The new will was duly drawn up and signed and witnessed.

This being achieved, the earl resumed his aimless wandering. Even during the night, the servants could hear him pacing backward and forward in his bedchamber.

One day when it was raining heavily, thin freezing iron rods of rain, the earl went out riding, despite protests from Morag and Cosmo. He rode a long way across the countryside, feeling weak and old, wishing for death for the first time and fearing its arrival.

The sound of a jaunty tune on the fiddle roused him from his gloomy reverie. He was approaching a small clachan, or village, little more than a huddle of houses and one muddy street.

The noise of the merry music struck up an answering stir in his heart. It was coming from a long low building. He dismounted and looked in the window. The villagers were celebrating a wedding and the celebrations were in their third day. Couples reeled and staggered to the wild music and the earl tapped his fingers appreciatively on the sill.

Then *she* danced past and looked over one saucy shoulder at him. She must have been all of thirty but she still had all her teeth. She had a tangled mane of black hair and her short skirts revealed dirty legs and bare feet. She was slightly cross-eyed and her mouth was full and red. "Dinnae staun there," she called out to the earl. "Come dance!"

And the earl did, leaping and hooching like an elderly Scottish satyr, and the company cheered and yelled and stamped their feet. He felt his youth return. Death fled to the horizon of his mind and he sat down, pulling his latest temptress onto his knee and drinking great gulps of whisky as if it were water.

"Come and dance," she cried again.

"Och, away wi' ye," groaned the earl. "I need a bit o' rest. I'm too auld."

"Too auld for everything?" she teased.

"I'm never too auld for that," grinned the earl.

"Prove it," she mocked. "Come outside."

"I'm your man," cried the earl, springing to his feet and pulling her laughing out into the rain, out into the cold, wet fields and behind a hedgerow.

As they lay down in the wet grass, she caught his earlobe between her strong teeth.

"Och," sighed the earl, "ye'll be the death o' me."

And she was.

Chapter Six

"Where's the little divil?" queried Mrs. Tallant, beating eggs with vigor.

Hamish looked up from the silver he was polishing and grunted, "Gone tae Perth wi' the mistress."

"Well, that's a mercy," snapped Mrs. Tallant. "Nae peace for us when he's around."

"He's a bonny lad," commented Hamish, brushing a speck of jeweler's rouge from his new livery, "but he gies me a fair scunner, him and his jokes." Both servants shook their heads dolefully over the misdeeds of the tenth Earl of Murr.

"He says tae me yesterday, he says," went on Hamish, " 'How exactly did my father die?' As if he didn't know. As if the whole county o' Perth didn't know. Whitna scandal that was!"

Seven years had passed since the death of the earl. The fact that he had died of a seizure during the throes of his last passion had been too good a story to keep quiet. It was a miracle that the secret of Roderick, Earl of Murr's birth had not been equally broadcast. But those that knew the truth of the young earl's parentage kept their mouths loyally shut — although they detested him one and all.

For young Roderick, known familiarly as Rory, was a pest, albeit a beautiful one. At the age of seven, he had long flowing golden curls and wide gray-blue eyes with a fascinating Celtic tilt that was almost oriental. He was sturdy and well-made and had infinite charm. He also had a great deal of intelligence which, since his overprotective "mother," Morag, Countess of Murr, considered him too young for boarding school or a tutor, taking charge of his education herself, found its outlet in a long series of ingenious practical jokes.

Only the day before had he put a mouse under the housekeeper's skirts as she was taking a pie out of the oven. Hamish had beaten him soundly and Rory had retaliated by writing, "Hamish loves Maggie Tallant" all over the castle walls.

Hamish had been elected to the official position as butler to her ladyship, with a fine livery to match. The menservants had received new footmen's livery in silver and scarlet and had been requested to powder their hair. The child must be surrounded with everything elegant, Morag had said.

And what of Morag after seven long years? She had grown in beauty, but it was a cold, still kind of beauty with little animation.

She had inherited great wealth from the earl and was extremely rich even by English standards. Suitors had flocked to the castle after the period of mourning was over and were turned down one by one. Morag was wrapped up in the care of the child, whom she had come to think of as her own. All the love in her love-starved life was poured on the child. In her doting eyes, Rory could do no wrong. And since Rory was equally devoted to Morag, he made sure that she never found out the worst of his tricks, and if she found out about any, he always had a charming excuse.

Morag had instigated many changes at Murr Castle. An architect had redesigned the chimneys so the rooms were well heated in winter. New plumbing had been installed and there was running water in a marble buffet outside the dining room. Carpets had been woven in Ayrshire to cover the stone floors and tapestries had been imported from Belgium to cover the walls. The stuffed pike had been given to Hamish, who, at first, did not know what to do with it, but had finally sold it at an auction in Perth and got drunk on the proceeds.

The castle wall had been moved half a mile to extend the gardens and a conservatory and succession houses had been built at right angles to the castle with a new servants' wing behind. Extra servants had been hired and Hamish proudly told his friends he was head of an army.

Lady Phyllis was eaten alive with jealousy.

The apartments in Edinburgh had been sold and Mr. James Murray, the lawyer, had advised selling the house in London since it would fetch a very good price. But somewhere in the back of

Morag's mind there was still a vision of a young man with black hair and green eyes and she felt if she sold the house, she would have admitted to herself that she would never go to London — never see him again.

She still led a fairly isolated life, and Rory had no friends — that she knew of — to play with since she considered the children of the local families not nearly good enough for her angel. She did not know that the enterprising Rory often slipped away from the castle when he was supposed to be in bed and played with the children of the local village, some two miles away. When he appeared at the breakfast table with purple shadows under his eyes, Morag would wring her hands and send for the doctor. Doctor McQueen would confirm her opinion that the child was delicate. Privately, the good doctor thought that Rory was as strong as an ox, but to tell her ladyship so would mean a curtailing of his frequent visits, and her ladyship paid well.

And so, for the most part, the world slipped by outside the castle walls unnoticed. Stories of the Peninsular War were duly reported in the newspapers as Wellington won battle after battle against Napoleon Bonaparte's troops. But the immediate daily concerns seemed more important. Wheat was fetching such a high price that Morag's extensive farmlands were almost doubling her fortune. Her fields were prosperous, her tenants well housed and her servants well fed. She was adored by one and all. Although her steward, Mr. Baillie, technically ran things, it was Morag who added the personal touch. Any sick tenant could expect a visit from her ladyship and a carriage full of comforts. Any bright child had his or her schooling paid.

Morag was queen of her small empire and almost content. But on the morning that Hamish and Mrs. Tallant were happily tearing the character of young Rory to pieces, two things happened which were to rend apart the quiet tenor of Morag's days.

Firstly, she bought a newspaper in Perth to read on the road home, a thing she had never done before, being completely uninterested in the outside world.

Rory was asleep beside her in the carriage, his fair head lolling against her arm. Morag's lady's maid, Scott, a recent acquisition, sat stiffly opposite.

Morag glanced idly through the pages until her eyes fastened on the social column. She idly read of the marriage of lord this to lady that — and then she felt a strange, apprehensive qualm. Marriage. Of course, he might already be married! She felt his presence so strongly, felt the feel of his lips against her own so vividly, he might as well have been in the carriage with her. All the hurt and longing which she had kept down over the years welled up and bubbled over.

She could go to London! Why had she never

thought of that! But the house was rented from year to year. "But it's *my* house," she thought, "and if I want to live in it, then I can." She looked at the paper again. There was the account of a ball at a certain Lady Pomfret's.

She found herself carefully studying the long description of the fashions and then looked down at her own serviceable clothes. She did so much walking and riding that she had had her clothes made accordingly; good, tough material in plain styles.

But it was ridiculous! There was dear Rory to think of. He should not be exposed to the dangers of London.

Did Lord Toby ever think of her? nagged the voice in her brain. Why had he left without so much as a good-bye?

She was a fool. He was probably happily married with, oh, twelve children.

The carriage rolled over the new gravel on the new drive up to the castle and Morag gently shook Rory by the shoulder. "We're here, dear. We're home. Wake up."

Rory struggled out of sleep, his face flushed, his eyes bright. Morag caught her breath. He was an incredibly beautiful child and she never tired of looking at him.

"Can I go and play, mother?" he yawned.

"No," said Morag with fond firmness; "dinner first."

Dinner had been moved to a more fashionable hour.

Grumbling under his breath, Rory climbed down from the carriage and waited outside the castle door for his "mother."

Suddenly there was the sound of a report and a bullet whined through his blond curls to bury itself harmlessly in the thick wood of the castle door. The horses plunged and reared. The footman leaped down from the backstrap and ran toward a spinney from which a pale wisp of smoke was rising. Hamish jerked open the castle door, "Whit was that, my leddy?" he cried. "I heard a shot."

Morag pushed past him, clutching Rory in her arms. "Someone tried to shoot Rory," she cried. "Quick, Hamish, have all the men out to search the grounds."

Her devoted servants scanned the countryside for miles round about. But of Rory's assailant, there was no sign. Mr. Baillie, the steward, was hastily called and gave his opinion that it was probably only a stray bullet from a poacher's gun. "Nobody would shoot the laddie," said Mr. Baillie, although he privately thought — "Shoot, no. Strangle, yes."

Rory had quickly got over his shock. He was inclined to agree with Mr. Baillie — having joined the local poachers some nights himself. He was desperate to escape to the freedom of the fields but his mother kept him close.

Like most children of his age, he had various small rituals which were important to him. One of the most important was that every evening, before dinner, he would go out beyond the castle walls and climb his favorite copper beech tree just as the light was fading. There he could sit, high up in its branches, looking over the rolling Perthshire countryside toward the distant blue mountains. He looked impatiently at his mother from under his long lashes as she sat over her embroidery.

"Mother, can I lie down before dinner?"

Morag stared at him. The poor child! He must indeed have received a bad shock.

"Of course, Rory," she said gently. "I will come up in a few moments to see how you fare."

"Oh, don't do that," said Rory. "I mean, I would really feel much better on my own and if I do not want your company, mama, then I do not want anyone's."

A glow of maternal love animated Morag's face. "Go then, darling," she said softly. "I will call you for dinner."

Rory walked slowly to the door and closed it very gently behind him. Then he fled. He escaped from the castle by his own secret way — a small little-used door in the cellars which led through tangled shrubbery to the back of the castle.

He dodged from bush to bush, moving as quietly as a shadow, frightened that one of the servants should see him and call him back.

Once out of sight of the castle, he slackened his pace. "I really must get mother to take me out of skirts," thought Rory, looking down miserably at his outfit. He was wearing an ankle-length frock with puffed sleeves and a high waist over long frilly pantaloons. On his curls was balanced a straw top hat — suitable perhaps for a child of five, thought Rory gloomily, but for a man of seven . . . !

When he reached his favorite tree, he began to climb with an incredible agility for such a small boy hampered by frilly pantaloons.

He now felt excited at the idea of having escaped death. He felt tremendously brave. He hesitated at his favorite perch and then decided, for the first time, to go higher. He dreamed of being a soldier and he climbed on up.

After all, drummer boys were little older than himself. He came out of his dream to realize that he was near the top of the tree, the branches were very thin, and he was a long way from the ground.

He looked down.

In the gathering dusk, the ground seemed to swing beneath him. The young buds had only just begun to sprout so he had an unimpaired view. Terror choked him and he clung to the tree for dear life. He could not go up, he could not go down.

He edged one chubby leg over a branch to take some of the strain off his arms and then clasped them tightly round the thin trunk of the tree.

But after only five minutes of this agony, he heard the hue and cry from the castle. He would be rescued — but then his mother would know he had tricked her and he would never be able to leave that way again. He was not a soldier. He was a coward. Rory's education, such as it was, had been given him by his mother — a little Latin, a little Greek and a great deal of romantic tales. None of his heroes would behave like this. He would get down — *and get down himself!*

As the sounds of the search grew nearer, he carefully and bravely freed one arm and jerked his dark blue dress up over his bright curls to hide them. His pantaloons were dark blue as well. With luck, he might not be seen.

The search passing by the very foot of the tree gave him all the courage he needed. As soon as the last dark figure had disappeared over the field and the last flaring, smoking torch had twinkled off into the distance, he began his cautious descent.

It was black night now and he could not see the ground. He seemed to have been edging down for a century until at last he felt the turf beneath his feet. He settled his topper at a jaunty angle on his head and skipped off toward the castle.

He crept quietly through the cellar door and then up a winding back stair to the first floor. He emerged onto the main landing and prepared to make a dash to the sanctuary of his room.

His mother was standing on the stairs, looking down. Morag gave a great cry and rushed forward, hugging him to her bosom, her frightened eyes taking in the blood smear on his face — a branch had scratched it — and the torn mess of his clothes.

"Rory!" she cried. "Dear God, what happened to you?"

Rory's fertile brain sprang into action. Not for worlds would he tell his mother he had lied to her.

"I went to my room like I said," he began, standing back from her and putting his hands behind his back. "But I felt dizzy and went outside the back of the castle for some fresh air . . . and . . . and . . . a man sprang out of the bushes and threw a sack ower — over — my heid — head."

"Dear God protect us!" wailed Morag. "What then?"

"I was slung on his back and carried off but the sack gave way and I fell oot — out. I ranandIranandIran," gabbled Rory now that this momentous lie was nearly at an end.

Had it not been for the earlier attempt, it is doubtful that even Morag would have believed this tarradiddle. But fear made her believe the worst. She called a council of war, and any servants who were not still out scouring the countryside for the boy were now sent out to look for the kidnapper.

By midnight, all the searchers had returned. There was no sign of any stranger in the area for miles around.

Panic-stucken, Morag slept in Rory's room that night with the small knife boy asleep on a

buckle bed outside the door. Rory bitterly re-
sented the guard supplied by the knife boy since
he was but little older than himself.

Morag's last waking thought was, "*Now* I
should go to London. Not for myself, but for
Rory."

But when the next day dawned bright and fair,
she wondered if she had been too precipitate in
her decision. But that day brought a visit from
Lord Arthur and his wife, who could barely con-
ceal their dislike of Rory. Morag talked com-
monplaces with them, her voice growing husky
as a nervous seizure caught at her throat. Of
course! Lord Arthur stood to inherit should anything happen to Rory. He wouldn't . . . he
couldn't. He might, said a niggling voice in her
brain.

Then arrived a letter from Cosmo, Laird of
Glenaquer. He had visited the castle several
times since the earl's death and had been profoundly shocked when Morag had put off her
mourning. He obviously expected her to wear
the willow for her husband until the day she
died.

"I trust you are comporting yourself well," the
letter ran, "and that Rory is behaving himself.
We must always watch that *doubtful family char-
acteristics* do not appear in the boy."

Morag bit her lip in vexation. Cosmo would
never let her forget the illegitimacy of Rory's
birth. Oh, to fly to London and leave them all!

She at last firmly made up her mind and, when

Cosmo's letter had gone up in the flames in the fire and Lord Arthur and Lady Phyllis had taken their leave, she drew Rory to her side, fondling his long golden curls.

"Rory," she began. "We have a fine mansion in London. I think perhaps a visit to the metropolis might be exciting. You will be able to see all the sights. What think you?"

Rory's mind rattled busily while his gaze merely reflected a limpid innocence.

"Shall I be allowed to have my hair cut and stop wearing petticoats?" he asked, after a long pause.

"You are too young yet, my son," said Morag fondly, thinking how enchanting he looked in his pretty dress and frilly pantaloons. "There is time enough to grow up."

Rory bit back the angry reply of, "Well, I won't go." He wanted to see the capital city and if he put his mind to it, something might be arranged. "I should like very much to go, mama," he answered in a clear, little voice.

"Then go we shall. Now send Hamish to me. I have much to discuss with him."

Rory did not allow the sulky expression which reflected his feelings to mar his face until he had closed the door behind him. He did not like Hamish. His mother was too familiar with this servant and relied too much on his judgment. Besides, Hamish had given him a beating.

Nonetheless, he crept quietly down the back stairs to the butler's pantry. No sign of Hamish.

Rory quietly opened the kitchen door and stood staring at the sight before him in glee.

Hamish was in the act of depositing a sly kiss on the new kitchenmaid's rosy cheek. He coughed and both swung around, Hamish turning a dull red and the kitchenmaid giving a saucy laugh.

"What is it?" demanded Hamish, who would never call the boy "my lord."

"My mother wants to see you," said Rory. "But I would like to talk to you first . . . alone."

Hamish sent the kitchenmaid about her business and turned and looked down at the child. Hamish wondered, not for the first time, what had happened to the innocence of childhood in Rory's case. It was like looking into the hard, flat, calculating eyes of a forty-year-old dwarf.

"Yes?" he barked.

"I don't think our good Mrs. Tallant would like to hear of your flirting with the serving wench," said Rory, twisting the hem of his dress between his chubby fingers.

"Why you . . ." began Hamish.

Rory nipped quickly behind a chair. "*Of course* I won't tell her, if you will do a very little thing for me."

"What do you want?" asked Hamish gruffly, thereby setting the small blackmailer's feet firmly on the first rung of his career. For, in truth, Hamish was very much in love with the stately, matronly housekeeper and hoped to marry her one day, the "Mrs." being a courtesy title. His flirtation with the kitchenmaid meant nothing.

Rory's eyes gleamed. "I simply want you to tell mama that I am too old to wear petticoats. We are to go to London and I want to wear my hair short as well. If you tell her, I shall not tell Mrs. Tallant."

Hamish hesitated. But the imperative summons of the bell sounded from the drawing room. "All right," he growled.

He went upstairs, muttering under his breath, "I'll kill that boy one day." But he composed his angry features before he opened the door and proceeded to persuade his mistress that young Rory should be out of petticoats.

"Oh, I do hate to see him grow up so quickly," she cried, and Hamish could only wonder at the love on her face. The horrible child was not even her own!

"But," went on Morag, "I am touched by your obvious concern for the boy. I know we don't often see eye to eye when it comes to young Rory's behavior because you are apt to take his childish pranks overseriously. You must not refine too much on the boy's innocent fun. But I will grant your wish, Hamish. Now let us discuss this proposed visit to London. I can do nothing until I speak to Mr. James Murray, but nonetheless . . ."

Rory slipped quietly down to the kitchens that evening, flushed with success. His mother was to take him to Perth the very next day to buy him a new suit of clothes and also to take him to the barber to have his locks shorn. The cook had been baking macaroons that afternoon. Ah, well, a little pressure on old Hamish and he could have as many as he wanted.

He opened the kitchen door.

Hamish and Mrs. Tallant were sitting side by side at the kitchen table with the teapot between them. Both looked up and stared steadily at young Rory.

"Come here, laddie," said Hamish at last.

Rory marched confidently forward.

Hamish reached out a long, muscular arm and put the struggling boy over his knee and proceeded to apply a leather slipper to Rory's wriggling bottom with great energy.

"Take that . . . and that . . . and that," said Hamish. "I told Mrs. Tallant all about the kitchenmaid and she forgives me. So *there*" . . . *smack* . . . "let that be a lesson tae ye" . . . *smack* . . . "and tell your mither by all means" . . . *smack* . . . "and I shall surely tell my lady why you got this thrashing."

He let Rory go. The boy was white-faced, his eyes blazing with such venom that, good Protestant though she was, Mrs. Tallant almost crossed herself. Then Rory turned on his heel and marched from the room. He did not cry until he had climbed high to the top of the castle and out onto the leads. Then he broke down, sobbing bitterly. Shame and rage engulfed him.

91

How could he have been so stupid? The next time, he vowed, he would have such a secret to hold over someone that they would not *dare* touch him.

In the weeks to come, Morag was busy with preparations for her departure. The main body of servants was to be left at the castle. Hamish, three grooms, two outriders and her lady's maid should make the journey south. The roads were considerably better than they had been seven years before so they would be able to travel all the way in the new, well-sprung traveling carriage.

Two days before their departure, two things happened. The newspapers announced the cessation of hostilities with France. The monster, Napoleon, was incarcerated on the island of Elba. And Miss Simpson arrived at Murr Castle. Rory was excluded from the room while she talked to his mother. He pressed his ear against the door but could only hear the soft murmur of voices. He did not know that Miss Simpson was begging for some sort of post in the household, her life having been hard after Morag's marriage. She had returned to her brother's farm where she had been treated little better than a servant.

Rory paced up and down until he was at last able to join his "mother."

He looked with undisguised contempt at the shabby governess.

"This is my old governess, Miss Simpson,"

smiled Morag. "Don't poker up, Rory. She is not here to instruct you. Miss Simpson is my new companion and will travel with us in London. Make your bow."

Rory, with his back to his mother, made Miss Simpson a low bow, and, as he looked up into her face, a slow, insolent smile played over his lips.

Miss Simpson folded her lips into a thin line and lowered her own eyes in case Morag should read the message in them.

For with Rory and Miss Simpson, it was a case of hate at first sight.

Chapter Seven

Lord Toby felt at ease with his conscience and the world — a pleasant and unusual state of affairs. He was seated in a trim drawing room in Grosvenor Square, waiting to propose marriage to one Miss Henrietta Sampson.

After a tumultuous and dangerous seven years, he could smile on the callow youth that had been himself and congratulate himself on having finally reached a stage of maturity. He was thirty-two years old and it was, after all, high time he grew up.

All that long time ago, he had eventually arrived in Perth after his horrible visit to Murr Castle, exhausted and feverish. His friends had prophesied correctly and there was no hope of making their way south until the spring. He had therefore ample time during a long convalescence to take inventory of his behavior.

He had tried to start up an affair with a married woman — something strictly against his code of manners and morals — and he was reaping the full benefit in feelings of disgust. As spring approached and he gradually grew stronger, Morag's picture changed in his mind's eye. Her mouth became full and voluptuous and her blue eyes, hard and calculating. By the time he and his friends were able to set out, she had retreated to the back of his mind, a beckoning, leering, red-haired harpy who had nearly stolen his love and his self-respect.

But on his return to London a strange feeling of unease stayed with him, and a dragging pain. The London Season bored him more than any previous Season he could remember. His life seemed to be that of an empty fribble. He bought himself a captaincy in a Hussar regiment and sailed for Spain to fight the devil within and the devils — in the shape of Bonaparte's massive armies — without.

Before the cessation of hostilities with France, he had caught a ball in the shoulder and had been invalided home. He emerged into society during the Little Season to find himself a great social success. He had always been noticed before, of course, due to his title and fortune. But he had been a good-natured young man, eager to please, and any one of the top ten thousand will tell you just how unfashionable these qualities are. He now presented a cold and arrogant manner to the world. He was, at best, coldly civil. He was accounted a splendid fellow.

It was at one of his first social occasions since he had recovered from his wound that he met Miss Henrietta Sampson.

She was of the Surrey Sampsons, an old family belonging to the untitled aristocracy. She had neat glossy brown ringlets and enormous brown eyes which she kept cast down.

Her nose was a trifle long and her chin a trifle square, but these things paled before her general air of calm good sense. She did not, of course, inspire passion but that was just as well, because passion was no good grounding for a marriage. Now on this day of the opening of the London Season, 1814, he had made up his mind. He would marry the fair Henrietta, retire to the country and farm his lands. He had no doubt but that the acceptance of his proposal lay entirely with Henrietta, her parents being a colorless couple without much say in anything.

He glanced out appreciatively at the masses of hyacinths in their trim windowboxes and at the pale, late spring sun gilding the trees of Grosvenor Square — for where else would such a correct lady as Miss Henrietta live but at the best address?

She entered the room very quietly and closed the door softly behind her.

He walked forward and took her mittened hands in his own, noticing in a satisfied way the demure gray of her dress and the neat bunches of ringlets — arranged, though he did not know it, to hide her rather large ears.

"You know why I am come, Miss Sampson." It was not a question.

"I think so," said Henrietta with a little half smile pinned to her mouth.

"I wish your hand in marriage, Miss Sampson.

You would make me the happiest of men. Please say 'yes.' "

"Oh, yes, Lord Freemantle," said Henrietta, still looking at the floor. "Papa told me you spoke to him yesterday and I took the liberty of sending an announcement of our betrothal to the *Gazette*."

Lord Toby frowned. That seemed to be taking a lot for granted. Then his brow cleared. It was just what he should have expected from his ever-practical Henrietta. She was so sane, so *English*. Now why had he thought that? What else could she be but English?

"You do me great honor," he said, smiling down at her. "May I kiss you, Henrietta?"

She blushed and raised her mouth to his. He pressed a chaste kiss on her pursed lips. Nothing happened to his senses, but, then, that should not surprise him since he hadn't expected anything to happen.

Henrietta drew back and at last raised her shining eyes to his. "I feel our marriage will be blessed," she cried, pointing upward to heaven with one finger in the manner of the saints in so many paintings. Lord Toby was suddenly and irresistibly reminded of the rude gestures of street arabs but grimly put the thought from his mind and drew her tenderly back into the circle of his arms, cradling her head against his chest.

He stared out of the window over her glossy ringlets, feeling immeasurably content.

A smart open carriage bowled past in the

square outside. The lady in it had been bending forward slightly to speak to a very beautiful little boy seated opposite. She raised a laughing face, seeming to look straight at Lord Toby. It was Morag, Countess of Murr, grown in years, grown in beauty, hair flaming under the saucy gold of a smart chip straw bonnet. Then she was gone.

She had materialized seemingly out of nowhere on this day of all days to shatter his peace. The red-haired leering harpy of his memories vanished. The blow of seeing her melted his frozen feelings, thawed out his icy social poise. He must recover his detachment. It could not have been her.

"You are hurting me!" cried Henrietta, pulling away and rubbing her arms where he had gripped them so tightly.

"Oh, my dear, I am sorry," he said, wrenching his mind to the present. "I shall call on you this evening to escort you and your parents to Almack's," he said gently. "You belong to me now, my darling."

"Yes," said Henrietta flatly. "Nothing will part us now. It would be breach of promise otherwise." She gave a merry laugh which tinkled in his ears like broken glass and added, at his look of surprise, "Stoopid! I was only funning."

Of course she was funning, he smiled to himself as he walked off around the square some ten minutes later. *Dear innocent little Henrietta! For a moment, she had made it sound like a threat!*

He made his way to Brooks's Club in St. James's Street, entered the black-and-white marble hall and made his way to the back morning room.

His friends, Alistair Tillary and Harvey Wrexford, had their heads buried in newspapers. The Honorable Alistair had grown fatter and chubbier than ever with the passing years and Mr. Harvey Wrexford so thin that it was said he could take cover behind a lamppost.

Alistair looked up from his paper, grinning with pleasure at the sight of his friend. "Saved myself a bit of money, Toby," he cried. "Been paying 'face money' for years and just learned this morning the club discontinued the practice five years ago. Someone might have told me, though."

The Dilettanti Society, which founded the club, passed a rule, "That every member of the Society do make a present of his Picture in Oil Colors done by Mr. Geo Knapton, a member, to be hung in the Room where the said Society meets."

Four years later there was another ruling which decreed that any member who had not provided a portrait should pay a guinea a year until it was delivered. These fines were known as "face money" and no one thought of stopping the custom till 1809.

"The club would vastly benefit from your portrait, Alistair," teased Lord Toby. "Mayhap there was not a canvas of large enough proportions."

"Shouldn't mock," grunted Alistair, eyeing his girth sadly. "Been on a diet, don't you see. Potatoes and vinegar. Nothing else. But the more I eat the cursed things, the thinner *Harvey* gets. Ain't no justice."

"Did she accept you?" asked Harvey Wrexford, lounging on the sofa. It was a great year for lounging and arranging one's limbs to their best advantage. One lounged on the carpet at the feet of the ladies, one lounged on sofas at one's club or one seated oneself at ease in a chair, placing the ankle of one leg over the knee of the other. This did not apply to the ladies, who were never supposed to touch the back of any chair, and the tyranny of that infernal machine, the backboard, still went on.

Lord Toby took off his curly brimmed beaver, having worn his hat for the regulation ten minutes. "Yes," he said, and then as if compelled, "It will be in the *Gazette* tomorrow."

"That's quick!" said Harvey, sitting up. "You must have been very sure of her reply."

"She was — rightly — sure of my proposal since I spoke to her father yesterday. Miss Sampson inserted the notice herself."

Both friends looked startled but good breeding forbade them from commenting on Miss Sampson's forward behavior.

Nonetheless Toby sensed their disapproval. "Miss Sampson is a very practical girl."

Alistair gave a noncommittal grunt. "I might try my luck with the new heiress," he said gloomily. "She's a widow so maybe she's not too fussy in men's looks." He tugged at his waistcoat which was riding uncomfortably up round the rolls of fat at his middle.

"Which new heiress?" demanded Toby. He was beginning to feel at ease with the world again. After what he had gone through at Murr Castle, it was natural that the sight of a beautiful redhead should upset him. It had not been she, of course. His imagination had played a trick.

"The Countess of Murr," said Alistair. "Didn't you know that family? As I 'member you went off to visit them that terrible winter and nearly killed yourself. You never did say what made you leave in such weather."

"I had outstayed my welcome," said Toby coldly, despite the racing of his pulses.

"Like that, was it?" said Harvey, writhing his long limbs in their skin tight pantaloons into a more comfortable position. "Not hospitable, eh."

"I do not like the Scotch," said Lord Toby repressively.

"Come, now," pursued Harvey. "The Old Prejudice is pretty much gone. But if that's the way you feel, you'll be the only man in London in no danger of losing your heart."

"This countess will be at Almack's this evening for the opening ball, no doubt?" said Lord Toby, studying the polish on the toe caps of his boots with great interest.

"Not she," said Harvey. "She don't go out in

society. All she cares about is that son of hers. Her courtiers are busy chasing her to Westminster Abbey and the Tower and Exeter 'Change. Young Lord Rotherwood stole a march on the rest of us by arranging a private tour of Madame Tussaud's."

"Us?" queried Toby, raising thin black brows. "Us, Harvey? Never say you have joined the pursuit of the Scottish widow."

Harvey looked so embarrassed and wiggled his limbs so frantically it seemed as if he were in danger of tying himself into a knot. "Can't remain a bachelor all m'days," he mumbled.

"How did her husband die?" asked Lord Toby.

"Great scandal evidently. He was much older than she . . . oh, forgot — you know the family. Well, he was making merry with a village maiden in the freezing rain and in an open field. Too much for him. Hadn't been a well man and it finished him."

"Would finish *me*," said Toby, affecting a boredom he did not feel. "Let us change the subject. Since my taste in amusements has long left the nursery, I am not likely to meet the countess."

"I really do not feel I am right in going," said Morag to her lady's maid, Scott, who was fastening the cross-tapes of Morag's chemise.

"It's an honor to receive vouchers for Almack's," said the maid in her prim, cultivated English accent in which slight traces of Scotch still peeped through like sprigs of heather on a rocky Highland escarpment. "Rory will do very well with Miss Simpson."

Morag sighed. She longed to go to Almack's Assembly Rooms. What female did not? In 1765 a Scotsman called William Macall reversed the syllables of his name to provide a more interesting title for his new assembly rooms, which became the most fashionable in London.

Now in this year of 1814, the rooms were ruled over by despotic patronesses whose word was law. To be seen at Almack's was to be an "Exclusive." To be refused vouchers labeled you a "Nobody." . . . and no Brahmin can shrink with more horror from all contact with a Pariah than an "Exclusive" from intercourse with a "Nobody." But there was Rory and there was Miss Simpson.

Miss Simpson had primly said she would, of course, be delighted to take care of Rory, and Rory had urged Morag to attend the ball. But Rory had been trying to hide a sort of wild glee and Miss Simpson seemed consumed by a slow-burning anger. Miss Simpson was too old to care for a clever high-spirited child like Rory, thought Morag unfairly.

Now that Morag was actually in London, her old dreams of Lord Toby had faded to the back of her mind. There were so many attractive young men to help her into her carriage and to send her flowers. She had been so young and inexperienced all those years ago.

He might be at the ball tonight, nagged a voice

in her brain, but she shrugged it away. There could be no comparison between that trembling green girl of the days of Edinburgh and the present dashing and sophisticated Countess of Murr.

Lord Freddie Rotherwood was the lucky gallant chosen to escort Morag to Almack's. He was sitting nervously in the drawing room of Morag's London home accompanied by Rory and Miss Simpson. The town house was of handsome proportions and had been decorated by the countess in the first stare. Various wild and kilted ancestors of the Murrs stared down at the elegant backless sofas, spindly chairs, and oriental rugs. A whole herd of stuffed trophies of the chase had been banished to the cellars where they loomed among the wine racks, their glass eyes never failing to give Hamish a shiver when he went down to choose the wine for dinner.

Lord Freddie sipped his claret appreciatively. He could not remember having tasted such a good wine. It is probable he had not. Many English aristocrats were unaware that their wine merchants fortified French wines with a great deal of brandy and some even slapped French labels on their own concoctions, one wine merchant having been found making and bottling Chateau Lafitte, vintage yesterday, on his own premises.

The late earl's wines had been imported directly from France and laid down long before the start of the wars.

Rory sat primly in the glory of dark blue velvet trousers buttoning onto a frilly blouse and eyed Miss Simpson from under his long lashes. He wanted her out of the room.

"Miss Simpson," he said finally. "I am desirous of a glass of water."

"Then ring the bell," snapped Miss Simpson.

"I want *you* to get it," said Rory mulishly. "You *are* supposed to be looking after me."

Miss Simpson rose wearily to her feet. She knew from experience that if she did not get it, Rory would retaliate by insulting her with cruel and personal remarks — if, as in the present case, his mother were absent.

Rory waited until she had closed the door behind her and turned his beautiful eyes on Lord Freddie. Lord Freddie was an engaging-looking young man, younger than Morag by two years. He had rosy cheeks and merry gray eyes and a good figure, although it was too sturdy to be fashionable.

"What have you brought me, my lord?" demanded Rory.

"Eh! What have I brought you?" repeated Freddie with an indulgent laugh. "Why, nothing, my little man."

"Then," said Rory icily, "it is high time you did."

Freddie stared at the boy in amazement. Only a bare minute ago, an angelic child had been facing him. Now he was confronted by a cunning dwarf with hard, calculating eyes. "Why should I bring you anything?" he demanded. "It ain't Christmas. It ain't your birthday."

"You are stupid," said Rory flatly. "My mother will not go with you if I take you in dislike."

"Why . . . why . . ." spluttered Freddie, "I have a good mind to put you over my knee."

Rory opened his cherubic mouth and then closed it quickly. Morag came into the room, and for the moment Freddie forgot everything else. She was wearing a tunic dress of white muslin edged with a gold border of Greek key design over a heavy white silk slip. Her red curls were dressed *á la victime,* and, as she moved toward him, he caught a breath of faint yet elusive perfume. She was a goddess, she was magnificent, she . . .

He was brought back from the groves of Arcadia with a bang.

"Mama," said Rory. "My head feels so hot and heavy."

Morag, who had stretched out her hand in greeting to the enraptured Lord Freddie, dropped it and rushed to Rory's side. "But you were very well not so long ago, my darling," she cried, kneeling down beside him and wrapping her arms around him. Rory stared steadily over her shoulder at Lord Freddie. "I don't know," he whined. "I suddenly feel so ill and weak. You must not leave me, mama."

"I should not dream of it, my precious lamb," cried Morag. "Lord Rotherwood will forgive me. Does your chest hurt?"

Lord Freddie took a shilling from his pocket and tossed it up and down. Rory looked at it with infinite contempt and said on a choked sob, "I-I ache so, mama. All over."

Lord Freddie sighed and took a guinea from his pocket and held it up. Morag still had her back to him and her arms round Rory. Rory rested his pointed chin on her white shoulder and gave Lord Freddie a brief nod.

"I ache *nowhere,* mama!" he cried with an enchanting, rippling laugh. "I was only funning and you believed me!"

Morag released him and gave him a mock slap on the bottom. "Is he not a scamp?" she cried, turning a glowing face to Lord Freddie. "You must not tease me so, Rory."

"I am sorry," said Rory with true contrition, for he hated to upset her in any way and it was all the fault of that fool Rotherwood being so slow on the uptake. Miss Simpson came in bearing the glass of water. "Why are you always bringing me glasses of water, Miss Simpson?" cried Rory merrily. "I declare, mama, she thinks I am a *whale!*"

Miss Simpson put the glass down on a side table and compressed her lips. She had long ago learned it was foolish to point out to Morag that her son was a malicious liar. Rory had all the weapons, all the answers. For a brief moment, the eyes of the old governess and the young lord met in complete understanding.

Then, "Go, mama, or you will be late," urged

Rory. "May I shake your hand, Lord Rother-wood?"

"By all means," said Lord Freddie gloomily as Rory palmed the guinea from his hand. "By all means."

Morag sat in the carriage in a fever of anticipation. This was to be the most *elegant* evening of her life. No crudity or vulgarity surely marred the hallowed halls of Almack's. She saw the whole thing in her mind's eye as some kind of celestial minuet.

No one had warned her of the circus *outside* Almack's.

There was an enormous press of carriages, fighting and jostling for space, urged on by their screaming passengers, frantic to a woman in case they did not gain entry to this social heaven.

Foolhardy coachmen would espy a small gap in the press and would drive both carriages and horses full tilt into the gap. The air was loud with the swearing of coachmen and grooms, shrieks from the ladies, and splintering wood. A cabriolet drove its shafts straight through the window of the coach next to Morag's.

"Is it always like this?" she gasped to her companion.

"Oh, always," replied Lord Freddie. "I mean, it isn't a fashionable event if you don't have to go through this, don't you see."

Morag's coachman, perched on his box, became impatient with the press and frightened for the safety of his horses. He let out a wild Highland battle cry which froze the struggling mass for a minute — long enough for him to see a sizable gap and drive his carriage in.

"Good work, Jimmy," called Morag and the coachman touched his cocked hat and grinned down at her. "I hope I get us back oot o' this mess, my leddy," he called. "Did ye ever see the like? Whitna clamjamfrey. But you go and enjoy yersel, my leddy."

Morag laughed and waved her hand. Lord Freddie stared at her in surprise. "Are your servants usually so familiar?" he asked.

"They are not familiar in the least," said Morag in chilly accents. "They merely display a native independence of character combined with genuine concern for my happiness."

"Sorry," mumbled Lord Freddie, privately thinking that his Highland rose was indeed set about with thorns in the shape of one impossible brat and an army of cheeky retainers.

Almack's was not so magnificent as Morag had expected. She had once been to one of the assemblies in Perth which had been held in an inn. It had been an infinitely more elegant setting than the one which now faced her. The ballroom was large and bare with a bad floor. Ropes were hung round it to divide the dancers from the audience of chaperones and wallflowers. Three equally bare rooms led off the ballroom where dry and tasteless refreshments were served.

But the magnificence of the guests more than

made up for these defects and the lighting and the music were good.

Morag was quickly surrounded by men, vying to partner her in the dances. As the evening wore on, she began to relax. Lord Toby would not come, of course. Not that she cared, but it would be interesting to see if he looked the same. Nothing more.

She was pirouetting gracefully under Lord Freddie's arm when she became aware of an old feeling of apprehension and unease.

Despite herself, her eyes were drawn to a corner of the room. Lord Toby stood there, staring straight across at her, those eyes, as green as she remembered, burning in his white face. He has changed, she thought breathlessly, tearing her eyes away. So much more elegant, so much more handsome, so much colder and harder.

"Dyed, of course," commented the calm voice of his fiancée at his elbow.

Lord Toby glanced down at Miss Sampson in some surprise. His Henrietta was not being spiteful, of course, merely making one of her practical observations.

"Do you refer to the Countess of Murr?" he asked.

"If that is she," said Henrietta, "the female with the impossible colored hair."

"I assure you it is not dyed," said Lord Toby. "I met the lady and her husband some seven years ago when I was touring Scotland. It is a dramatic color, I admit, but quite usual in the Highlands of Scotland."

"Poor girl! How unfortunate!" said Henrietta, with a complacent pat at her brown curls. "But then she is newly come to town and will learn that *dark* beauties are the fashion. She is quite mature of course and perhaps I should advise her to wear caps."

"As I remember, she is some two years older than you, Miss Sampson," said Lord Toby with some asperity.

"Really!" Henrietta fanned herself languidly. "It must be the rigors of the climate."

Lord Toby looked back at Morag. Her figure was now full-breasted and mature. She moved with an ethereal grace, and more than one man stared at her hungrily.

He was suddenly angry that she could laugh and dance with such seeming unconcern. She had seen him, after all. Surely she remembered him. Well, he was not likely to find out. He knew she was probably already bespoke for every dance. An elderly gentleman came to claim Henrietta's hand for the cotillion and left him free to go in search of his friends.

He found the Honorable Alistair in a secluded corner clutching one puffy ankle, his chubby face rather white.

"Wrenched it," said Alistair gloomily. "And I am supposed to dance the waltz with the beautiful countess. Could you find Harvey for me? I would ask you to take my place but you've got that cursed prejudice against the Scottish race."

"I shall take your place," said Lord Toby and turned away abruptly, leaving Alistair with his mouth open.

Morag was promenading round the ballroom with Lord Freddie in an interval between dances. Neil Gow and his fiddlers struck the opening bars of the waltz and Morag curtsied to Lord Freddie and turned to look for the Honorable Alistair. She gave a little gasp as she found the green eyes of Lord Toby Freemantle glinting down at her.

"Mr. Tillary . . . ?" she said in an almost pleading voice.

"He has twisted his ankle," replied Lord Toby, "and has begged me to replace him."

Morag moved wordlessly into his arms. Lord Toby looked bitterly down at the top of her glowing curls as he whirled her round in the steps of the waltz. She had no right to look so enchanting. He wanted to shake her. To shout at her. To demand an explanation.

"Why?" came a soft whisper from his partner.

He stumbled slightly with surprise and looked coldly down into her blue eyes. "Why, what?" he demanded rudely.

"Why did you leave without saying good-bye?"

Toby stared at her. He was tempted to snap that he hadn't the faintest idea what she was talking about. Instead he said, "Do not remind me of the follies of my youth, madam. I have since learned that to attempt to seduce another man's wife — however willing she may be — is pretty bad sport."

Morag stopped abruptly, face aflame. "There are more ways of abusing hospitality than you think, my lord," she said in a low voice. "Breaking hearts is one of them." She turned on her heel and left him standing in the middle of the floor. He was unaware for a few moments of the staring, curious faces. "Breaking hearts." What had she meant? She could not possibly mean . . .

His heart beat hard and fast and he felt a suffocating lump in his throat. He must follow her and ask her. He started across the ballroom in her direction, unaware that he had just received one of the biggest set-downs that Almack's had ever seen.

But before he could reach Morag's side, his fiancée was at his elbow, her eyes snapping with curiosity.

"What a monstrous thing to do!" she exclaimed. "What *mauvais ton*. And to cut you in Almack's of all places. How dare she!"

For the first time, Lord Toby became aware of a circle of staring curious eyes. "I said something unforgivable to Lady Murr," he said in a clear, carrying voice. "I shall call on her tomorrow to apologize."

There was a little sigh of disappointment from his listeners. It was a storm in a teacup, that was all.

"How noble of you! How brave!" cried Henrietta. "To take the blame when all the world and his wife knows my lady is a trifle *farouche*."

Lord Toby pulled her angrily away from their audience and did not open his mouth until he had found a quiet corner.

"Don't be so vulgarly jealous," he said icily.

Henrietta stared at him in amazement. Never had he used such a tone of voice to *her*. Others, yes, for he was famous for his set-downs. She opened her mouth to say something cutting but decided at the last moment to change her tactics and burst into tears instead.

Lord Toby stifled a feeling of impatience. Where had his serenity of the morning gone? Only that morning the idea of making this girl his wife had seemed such a desirable — an eminently sensible — thing to do.

"Don't cry," he said wearily. "I cannot abide watering pots. I like you for your calm good sense, Miss Sampson . . . Henrietta. Come, my love. Dry your tears and I tell you what I will do for you. You know you are desirous of going to the Montclairs' breakfast tomorrow. Then I shall escort you."

Morag glanced over her partner's shoulder and saw the girl with the brown ringlets turn a glowing face up to Lord Toby. Her heart felt like a lump of ice in her bosom.

"Who is that girl with Lord Freemantle?" she asked Harvey Wrexford who was partnering her. Harvey twisted his long neck around. "Oh, that's Toby's fiancée," he said carelessly. "Announce-

114

ment's in the newspapers in the morning. Managing sort of female, but Toby's a cold fish where women are concerned . . . more of a man's man, don't you see."

Morag nodded dumbly. She wanted to go home and hug Rory and then go to bed and lay her aching head on a cool pillow.

What a truly terrible evening!

What a truly terrible evening, thought Miss Simpson. Rory had had the time of his life at her expense. He had greedily ordered all sorts of goodies from the kitchen and had rounded off the evening by demanding wine. Grimly Miss Simpson had given it to him and had awaited the expected result. Rory had blinked several times like an owl and then had fallen fast asleep.

After she had put him to bed, she returned to the drawing room and sat deep in thought. She had never told Morag the full extent of Rory's villainy. Miss Simpson was terrified at having to return to her brother's farm and she was sure that Morag would send her away were she to complain of Rory. She was too old to find another position. But she ached to see Rory punished as he deserved, and the only person who could hurt him was his mother.

All children in Miss Simpson's care — including Morag — during her long years governessing had been in her complete charge and, sad to say, she had bullied them mercilessly.

Morag had not forgotten that bullying — of

115

that Miss Simpson was sure. For although Morag was soft-hearted enough to supply her with the post of companion, she had made it quite clear that Miss Simpson was to have no authority over Rory.

Miss Simpson cracked her bony knuckles and came to a decision. She would *write* to Morag, a clear and lucid letter. She could put it better that way since she hardly ever managed to see Morag without Rory being somewhere about.

Then that hell's spawn would receive the whipping he deserved!

Chapter Eight

Lord Toby Freemantle walked slowly in the direction of Albemarle Street to pay his respects and offer his apologies to the Countess of Murr. He began to wonder if she would even see him.

Forget about the rights and wrongs of the matter, it was old history and he had had no right to insult her. And if he did not find what she had meant by "breaking hearts" he would be unable to rest. Once he had received her explanation, he convinced himself, the ghost would be laid and he would be free to resume his placid if somewhat boring existence.

Although it was early afternoon, the day held a harsh bright glitter and a rising wind whipped pieces of paper round in miniature whirlwinds in the cobbled streets.

He paused for a moment to watch the splendid sight of the Sun Insurance Fire Brigade tearing into action, brass bells clanging, great horses straining, and the firemen in their leather helmets, striped stockings and blue coats clinging to the engine's side. The freshening wind whipped this way and that, tugging at his hat and playing in the snowy folds of his cravat.

A huge butler with the pale gray narrow eyes of the Highlander answered the door to him and accepted his card with a clumsy bow. He was shown into a small saloon on the ground floor which was tastefully decorated in shades of green and gold.

After some minutes, he became aware that he was not alone. A beautiful child was lolling in a chair in the corner of the room. Rory and Lord Toby surveyed each other in silence. Rory was feeling queasy after his debauch of the night before.

"Are you come to see mama?" he asked.

"Yes," said Toby, feeling a strange pang and wondering what on earth was the matter with him. Morag had been married after all. It was only natural she would have a child. He now realized that despite all the old earl's winks and hints, he had in his heart of hearts believed Morag to be virginal. He must have been mad.

"Are you Lord Toby Freemantle?" queried Rory, swinging his feet listlessly over the edge of the chair.

Lord Toby stared at the child in surprise. "Yes, I am. How did you guess?"

"Green-eyed sneering dandy," said Rory vaguely. "You've got such green eyes I thought she must have meant you."

"Has anyone ever told you you are an insolent young pup?"

"Frequently," replied Rory with great indifference.

Lord Toby studied the child narrowly. Rory felt too ill to put on his usual angelic expression. He was too tired to think of any blackmailing tricks and so Toby was one of the few people to see Rory for what he was — his better side anyway — a frighteningly high intelligence starved for an outlet.

"I supposed you are cramming for Eton," said Lord Toby.

"No," sighed Rory. "I am too young and charming to be sent away among a lot of rough boys."

"You should not mock your mother."

"I! Never!" cried Rory hotly. "But I would like to learn, oh, so many things. Mother teaches me, you know. But it's mostly romantic stories which were all very well when I was a boy, but now I am a young man," added eight-year-old Rory loftily, "such things bore me."

"You do not need to fret over your lack of education," said Toby gently. "There are plenty of books, you know. You can educate yourself."

"Really!" said Rory with a languid, affected drawl which grated on Lord Toby's nerves. "Pray tell me, if you were my tutor what books would you have me read?"

"Books on steam engines, sailing ships, and horses. Books of travel describing far countries. Books of shells and birds and insects."

Rory's eyes gleamed and he sat up. He was as starved for fact as his "mother" had been for fiction.

The door opened and Hamish entered. "I am afraid her ladyship is not available," he said.

Lord Toby bowed his head. "I see. Present my compliments to her ladyship and my apologies. Lady Murr will understand."

"Very good, my lord."

Hamish moved to show Lord Toby out but Rory sprang to his feet. "Lord Freemantle is *my* guest," he cried. "Pray leave us!"

Hamish ignored Rory and moved to the double doors which led from the saloon into the main hall.

Rory stared at Lord Toby with pleading eyes.

Lord Toby did not find Rory charming but he found the child's intelligence fascinating. He made up his mind.

"Leave us, please, a few minutes," he said, turning on Hamish a singularly sweet smile.

"Very well," grunted Hamish. "But I hope your lordship knows what he is about."

He went out and closed the doors behind him.

"Now," said Rory, all his languor gone, "if you will buy me these books you describe, I will arrange a meeting with my mother."

Lord Toby's face hardened. "No, my little blackmailer. You may ask your mother to take you to a bookseller."

"I can make things very difficult for you," pointed out Rory.

"No, you can't," said Lord Toby. "There is nothing you can do except slop around feeling vastly sorry for yourself and cramming your mouth with sweetmeats and getting spots on your face."

"My skin is beautiful," cried Rory, dancing up and down on a chair in front of the looking glass over the fireplace in an effort to see his face. There was one spot, he eventually noticed, right on his forehead.

Tears of anger filled his eyes. But no one else had ever understood him as well as this tall, handsome lord who stood watching him indifferently.

He suppressed his anger and climbed down from his chair. "We could deal extremely well together, my lord," he said, turning the full blast of his charm on Lord Toby.

"There is no reason why we should," rejoined Lord Toby, picking up his hat and cane. "Now I must be off. I am to attend the Montclairs' breakfast and my fiancée will never forgive me if I am late."

Rory, in a last effort to please, rushed and held the doors open for him. But Lord Toby did not even notice. He did not, after all, know that Rory normally never held doors open for anyone other than his mother.

After Lord Toby had left, Rory sat down and stared moodily into space. A glimmer of an idea formed in his brain. For the first time in his life, he wanted someone to like him. And that someone was Lord Toby. He stood on tiptoe and ran his fingers through the cards on the card rack on the mantelshelf. Ah, here it was! An invitation to the Montclairs' breakfast. Why did things called "breakfast" always begin at three o'clock in the afternoon? He extracted the invitation and went in search of his mother.

Morag was feeling tense and nervous. She wished now she had seen Lord Toby. But he was engaged and she didn't like him anyway and he was rude and unkind and why did she care so desperately?

Her face lit up with affection as Rory came tripping into the room, the invitation card behind his back.

"I was talking to Lord Freemantle," he began, "and he said I should read books on, oh, all sorts of things like steamships and horses."

"Anything that man says is bound to be wrong," snapped Morag. "You will learn enough hard facts later in your life without addling your brains at this early age."

Rory sighed. He was losing his touch. He should simply have asked her for the books without mentioning Lord Freemantle's name. He changed his tactics.

"Look, mama. I have a spot on my forehead."

"Only a little one, my love. You eat too many sugar plums."

"I think it is a lack of fresh air, mama. I miss the country so much," said Rory who did not miss it in the slightest and found the crowded streets of the city vastly more entertaining.

"Do you, my son?" asked Morag, feeling a sudden stab of conscience. "We cannot return to

Perth, you know, until the mystery of your assailant is solved. My steward is investigating the matter. Perhaps we could take a drive this afternoon."

Rory whipped out the breakfast invitation. "You have *this*, mama. My name is on the invitation also and only see, it says in the corner that there are to be fireworks. Only think, mama. Fireworks!"

"Very well," said Morag. "Run along and tell Miss Simpson she is to accompany us and then send a footman round to the stables with a message. I did accept the Montclairs' invitation but I did not mean to go since I feel so tired today. But if your heart is set on it . . . ?"

"Oh, *yes*."

"Then tell Miss Simpson that we leave in an hour."

Rory skipped up the stairs to the governess's room and crashed in without knocking. Miss Simpson had been in the act of finishing her catalogue of Rory's iniquities. She blushed and put her large hands quickly over the letter. Rory flicked a glance at the paper on her desk and carefully looked away as he delivered his message. So what was old Simpers up to? Whatever was in the letter, she would not have time to finish it now. And wherever she hid it, Rory would find it.

Sir Eric and Lady Felicity Montclair held the breakfast at their *cottage ornée* in Surrey. The cottage was in fact a large sprawling villa, all its rooms being designed in the same manner, flesh-colored stucco and gold, and curtains of crimson and white silk. The effect was rather florid and grandiose. The grounds, however, were delightful with many pleasant walks and arbors. Tables for the guests had been set out on the smooth lawns. It was still quite windy and the light pastel muslins of the ladies fluttered across the grass like so many flowers.

Henrietta Sampson walked by the side of Lord Toby Freemantle and gracefully accepted felicitations on her forthcoming marriage. After some time, it dawned on her that her tall companion was emanating an atmosphere of unease. Henrietta remembered her comments on the Countess of Murr at Almack's the night before and wondered if that had offended her fiancé. Men were so strange! They said the most frightful things about each other but let only one miss pass a derogatory remark about another female and she was labeled a shrew. Henrietta resolved to be extremely pleasant to the young Countess of Murr should their paths cross again.

Unfortunately this good resolution lasted only as long as her first glimpse of Morag. Henrietta was wearing a new poplin tunic gown in a flattering straw color. She felt it became her well. But that wretched countess was also wearing a tunic gown in the same color and it set off her creamy skin and flaming hair to perfection.

Henrietta felt pale and dowdy by comparison.

Lord Toby's rather cold, arrogant face was hardly to be expected to delight the eyes of a child. But Rory brightened immediately at the sight of his new hero and he tugged Morag impatiently toward Henrietta and Lord Toby.

Morag had been talking to Miss Simpson and had allowed Rory to tug her along. She realized with a start that Lord Toby was bowing before her while the lady at his side was raking her eyes up and down Morag's dress with a singularly unpleasant stare.

Lord Toby felt that to offer Morag an apology in front of his fiancée would not be a good idea at all. He was uncomfortably aware that his pulses were racing with a strange, heady excitement. Morag made him a stiff little curtsy and said, "Come, Rory," and without waiting to see whether he followed her or not, walked away. Just then, Henrietta's mother, Mrs. Lydia Sampson, came fluttering up. She was dressed in shades of gray and lilac and looked like a wispy insubstantial ghost. "Henrietta," she whispered. It was not a secret she had to impart. Mrs. Sampson always whispered. "The hem of my gown has come loose. You are so clever with a needle, my dear. Pray walk with me into the house and assist me."

Henrietta assented with bad grace. One of her favorite roles was that of Dutiful Daughter and she felt obliged to play it one more time.

"I shall return quite soon," she said, squeezing

Lord Toby's arm. "Oh, here is that wretched child again."

"Go along with you, Miss Sampson," said Lord Toby, wondering why he found it so hard to call her by her first name. "I am well able to deal with a child."

As soon as Henrietta had left with her mother, Rory, who had been hanging about hopefully a little way away, came scampering up.

"Well, young man," said Lord Toby severely. "Who are you blackmailing today?"

"No one as yet," replied Rory calmly. "My mother's suitors have not approached me yet."

"What a horrible brat you are! Has it never dawned on you that people might help you out of sheer good nature?"

"No," said Rory simply. "Good nature is not fashionable. I am told 'It will never *do*.' "

"You must not follow the sillier dictates of society or you will become quite inhuman. Have you heard the story of the famous dandy who was walking along the riverbank with his lady friend. No? Well, there was a man drowning in the river and the lady knew the dandy to be a powerful swimmer. 'Pray, sir,' she cried. 'Why do you not rescue that poor gentleman.' Whereupon the dandy raised his quizzing glass and surveyed the drowning man and said in accents of horror, 'But, my dear young lady, we have not been introduced.' "

Rory laughed gleefully. "Yes," commented Lord Toby dryly, "I thought that might amuse you. Where did you come by these odd blackmailing tactics, my soulless dwarf. It's not as if anyone ever blackmailed you."

"Oh, yes they did," said Rory, falling into step beside him. "In Perthshire, you know, I used to slip out of the castle at night and go to the village to join the boys in their games. But they used to laugh at me because I was in petticoats. I asked them when would they stop teasing me and let me join in their games, and they said, 'Why, when you give us something to keep us quiet.' I didn't have any money but I used to steal biscuits and sugar plums and take them with me and as long as I had something to give them, they would let me play with them for a little. You must not tell my mother, though. I trust you are a man of honor?"

"Word of a Freemantle," said Toby, looking down at the boy curiously. "I don't know what else you could expect," said Toby after a pause. "The village children knew you were rich and an earl. They probably had little themselves. There must have been boys of your own station in life to play with."

"No," said Rory. "I mean, there were, but mama thought them too rough."

"And what of sports, hunting and fishing?"

"I am considered too delicate."

"But surely you had some friend among the servants. At your age, I followed one of my father's grooms about like a dog."

A shadow crossed Rory's usually calm face.

"Hamish!" he said bitterly. "He hates me. I mean, even before I blackmailed him he didn't like me. He's our butler."

"Hamish, too," murmured Lord Toby, but Rory had never known anyone to listen to him like this before and would not be checked.

"Hamish looks at me in *such* a way and once when I asked him why he did not call me 'my lord,' he gave a very nasty laugh as if he knew something about me that I would not like. Mrs. Tallant — our housekeeper — is the same. There is a lack of respect. . . ."

Lord Toby stopped and swung the boy around to face him. "Now, listen to me, young man, you have gained a very warped view of life. People treat you as you treat them. Try to be kind. Try to talk to Hamish, for example. Respect must be earned."

"Run along, you tiresome child." Rory had been staring wonderingly up at Lord Toby, trying to assimilate these new ideas when this grating, female voice cut across his reverie. Henrietta was back. "I said, 'run along,' " she snapped. "Really, Toby, I don't know what Lady Murr must be thinking of. Bringing a child along."

Rory raised his large, limpid eyes to Henrietta's face and said in his clear soprano, "You are jealous of my mother. She is very beautiful."

Up till that minute, Lord Toby had had no idea that his Henrietta had a waspish temper.

She had always — until last night anyway — been sweet and smiling and docile.

"How dare you?" screamed Henrietta. "As if I would be jealous of a *Scot*. Heathenish savages. They should be exterminated!"

Rory's eyes flashed hate mixed with malice and then he scampered off. Lord Toby felt quite rigid with shock.

"Hear this," he said quietly. "You are never to raise your voice in my presence again. That was extremely cruel. You will go to Lady Murr and apologize for your behavior, which was totally unreasonable."

The wheels and cogs of Henrietta's mind churned and turned rapidly. She knew she had gone too far. She knew what she must do.

"Oh, Toby," she sighed. "Of course I shall apologize. I am so much in love with you that it makes me behave badly."

Lord Toby should have been gratified to hear his beloved's pretty, docile apology. He should have been angry at Morag for her chilly acceptance. But his thoughts were in confusion and he felt strangely trapped. The pressure of Henrietta's little hand on his arm began to feel like a manacle.

With all the acute perception of the child, Rory recognized Henrietta's apology for what it was — a wile to charm Lord Toby.

He felt hurt and restless and when he felt hurt and restless, he craved mischief as an addict will crave his card game or his opium.

After the meal had been served, the guests were invited to view the rooms of the Montclairs' new cottage. Despite its title of "cottage," it was large enough to house at least four farmers, their families and their laborers. The guests crowded into the drawing room, which looked exactly the same as the other rooms, with one exception. A newly painted portrait of Lady Montclair hung over the fireplace. In the painting she was dressed in her best purple silk with her ample bosoms well hitched up. A purple turban ornamented her head and her small mouth was fashionably pursed and slightly open.

Lady Montclair stood under her portrait and complacently awaited the expected compliments. She slowly became aware that her guests were staring at it with expressions of shock on their faces. She turned around and looked up. And then fell into a swoon, her husband leaping forward to catch her just in time.

Someone had drawn a balloon from the portrait's painted mouth and in the balloon, neatly painted in black, one vulgar, shocking four-letter word.

Lord Toby looked across the room. Rory was standing with his little hands folded and a pious expression of shock and bewilderment on his angel face.

"Now I know what makes you tick, young man," thought Lord Toby with a strange mixture of anger and pity. Anger that the boy could be so cruel, pity for his narrow, overprotected life.

If only Henrietta would release her clutch on his arm for one minute, then he would be free to talk to Morag.

The guests had been treated to a French play and a Tyrolean concert and were once again promenading in the gardens before the start of the proposed ball which was to be held at the conservatory at the back of the house.

Still with Henrietta clamped to his side, Lord Toby walked sedately through the failing romantic light of dusk and wished he could escape. He had quite suddenly taken her in dislike and did not know what to do about it. He could not propose to a girl one day and hate her the next! If only she would leave him for a minute so that he could arrange his thoughts.

"Oh, look at that pretty fountain!" cried Henrietta, leading him toward a shallow basin in the center of which a merman held a spouting dolphin. Lord Toby stopped dutifully and stared at the merman. The dolphin, he noticed idly, spouted water by means of a thin copper pipe passing through its tail and up through its mouth. He frowned. He could have sworn a white hand, glimmering in the dusk, had twitched at the pipe.

The next minute, Henrietta screamed. The water from the dolphin's mouth, instead of spouting up into the air as usual, was suddenly directed straight at her, soaking her from head to foot in a matter of seconds.

Lord Toby darted off to the other side of the fountain but there was no sign of anyone. A crowd attracted by Henrietta's screams began to gather. Mrs. Sampson led her weeping daughter off to the house.

And Lord Toby was free.

He went immediately in search of Morag. At first he could not find her anywhere among the guests and so he wandered farther into the gardens and away from the house. Then he saw a faint glimmer of a straw-colored dress over by a clump of larch. She was alone.

The blustery wind had died and the evening was calm and still.

He walked quickly up to her, afraid that she would disappear. He rehearsed all sorts of formal openings to conversation in his mind and ended up by simply saying, "Morag."

She swung round and looked up at him. She had removed her pretty bergère bonnet and was holding it in her hand by the strings. Her hair glowed like rich mahogany in the fading light.

"I received your apology, Lord Freemantle," she said hurriedly, looking down. "You have changed," she added in a low voice.

"Changed? I? In what way?"

"You have become harder. I have watched you in company today. You are often almost rude. It is the fashion, I know, but somehow I thought you would be above the dictates of fashion. There is a want of sympathy . . ."

"Enough!" he cried. "I am grown older and

wiser, that is all." He looked down at her. He had wished to speak to her about her son. The boy should go to school or at least have a tutor. He needed the company of fellows of his age before he turned into a precocious calculating monster. In fact, thought Lord Toby grimly, he already *was* a precocious monster. He was about to tell her so when he realized she was trembling and that her face was quite pale.

He found himself saying, "*Why*, Morag? I went to your room and you were not there. It was very wrong of me, I admit, for you were married. But to agree to see me and then fly to make noisy love with your husband . . ."

"I have never . . ." began Morag and flushed.

She had been about to say that she had never made love with her husband. But then, how could she account for the presence of Rory? Instead she said in a suffocated voice, "My lord called for me. He was in great pain. He wished me to pull a tooth for him . . . which I did. It was very difficult to get it out and it took some time. I had to get up on the bed and kneel over him and pull as hard as I could, and . . ."

She stopped amazed as Lord Toby let out a great shout of laughter. Those words and noises and bed creakings which had burned like fire into his brain all those years ago were now very simply explained. At last he stopped laughing and said almost dreamily, "And when you had got it out, the earl said, 'Och, Morag, my love, my precious. Naebody could ha' done that like you.' "

"Yes, something like that," said Morag.

"But don't you see what I thought from hearing that?" cried Lord Toby.

"Oh," said Morag after a moment, with a slight blush. "Not that evening," she continued in a small, chilly voice. The secret of Rory's birth must be kept at all costs.

Her words hurt but he had to admit that again he was behaving badly. The earl had been her husband, after all.

"I gather congratulations are in order," Morag continued, throwing more ice on his fire.

"Yes," he said flatly. "Thank you."

Lord Toby thought wearily that he should put a good word in for Rory to prove to the boy, if nothing else, that at least someone was prepared to help him without being forced to do it.

"My Lady Murr," he began in formal tones when Morag gave a little cry and started as some small nocturnal animal ran across her foot. She stumbled and fell heavily against him.

Lord Toby's social poise, his arrogance, his coldness melted away and before his brain could relay any warning to his churning emotions, he had caught her in his arms and was desperately kissing her hair, her nose, her ear as she struggled and tried to escape.

He muttered something incoherent under his breath and forcing her chin up pressed his mouth violently down on her own. He wrapped his arms tightly round her, moulding her body against his own. He felt he was being driven crazy with a mixture of intolerable lust and a burning sweetness.

Her initial resistance was gone and she kissed him back with a strangely innocent passion. She was wearing that elusive perfume which smelled of a mixture of heather and the summer wind.

At last he drew away, his green eyes glinting down at her in the pale light of a rising moon. Her mouth was bruised and swollen and her lips were trembling.

"Oh," she cried, putting a shaking hand to her mouth. "You are *faithless!*" And with that, she turned and fled, leaving him standing, staring after her.

What on earth could she mean? She was no longer married.

Henrietta! Morag was free. But he was not. Hell and damnation! He had forgotten Henrietta!

Rory awoke and stared around, confused for a moment. Then he remembered where he was. He had fallen asleep on a small sofa in a corner of Lady Montclair's drawing room. He shifted lazily against the silken cushions, wondering vaguely why his mother had not come in search of him.

Then he heard a vague murmur of voices. One of the voices, a man's, sounded vaguely familiar but he could not place it immediately. His mother had so many admirers.

The sofa on which he was lying was tucked

into a recess at the window so he was concealed from the room. He would wait until whoever it was went away. He felt too tired to cope with the inevitable adult questions about why he was not at school. Then the man's voice, the familiar one, rose slightly. "The Corsican fishermen are loyal?" it said.

Then another man replied in French — no doubt one of the French actors from the play.

The familiar voice spoke again.

"The fact that I am English makes no odds. You think I am doing it for money, my dear chap. True enough. But I am loyal to Boney, have no fear . . ."

The voices faded away and he lay very still. How strange.

Then he heard his mother calling him.

He slid down from the sofa and ran to the door of the drawing room.

Morag looked very white and strained. "I was asleep, mama," he cried. "Do not look so worried. I was tired but some men talking woke me."

He thought he heard a sudden indrawn hiss of breath and swung round. But there were various familiar faces in the crowd, crossing and recrossing the hall. He forgot about it immediately. He wanted to go home as soon as the firework display was over.

Morag was strangely quiet on the road home but Rory was too sleepy to care. He felt he could sleep for a whole day.

Soon they were moving through the still-busy

streets of London. Morag, who had been gazing idly out of the carriage window, gave a sudden exclamation. "Do but look, Miss Simpson," she cried. "That little child."

Miss Simpson followed her pointing finger. Although it was midnight, there was almost as much traffic as there was at midday. Through the coaches and carriages drove a small boy. He must have been only twelve years old. He was quite alone and driving a small cart pulled by a large dog, which he tooled with masterly ease through the press of carriages.

"All alone!" said Morag in wondering tones.

"Nothing so strange in that," said Miss Simpson wearily. "In this country, ma'am, the children are men at eight and hanged at twelve."

Rory stared with envy after the disappearing child. Morag held him very close. Lately she had begun to worry that she was perhaps overprotective toward Rory. But now she was sure she was doing the right thing. Children seemed to become adult so soon, and childhood was a precious thing. Rory should be protected for as long as she could possibly manage.

Chapter Nine

Rory was awake before anyone else and the first thing he remembered was that letter Miss Simpson had been writing. He dressed himself and ran downstairs. The morning's post had not yet arrived but there was a sealed letter lying on the half table in the hall on the silver tray which had been placed there for calling cards.

He looked around quickly. No one.

He picked up the letter and scampered back to the safety of his room. He cracked open the seal and quickly read the contents, his eyes widening as he read a concise catalogue of his sins.

An idea started to form in the back of Rory's brain. He read the letter again. Miss Simpson had made no reference to her own position in the household.

Dear Lady Murr,

Do not consider me Presumptuous. I am writing these unwelcome Facts for your Own Good. Rory is spoilt beyond Comprehension. He accepts Bribes from your callers, desirous of seeing you. He tells Lies. He drew that Un-mentionable Word on poor Lady Montclair's portrait, for one of the maidservants told me.

I pray you, before his character has become Degenerate beyond recall, see that he is soundly whipped as he deserves. It is often better to be Cruel in Order To Be Kind. Such Sins if not beaten soundly out of a child, foment and nourish.

I have nothing more than yr Best Interests at Heart.

Yr Humble and Obedient Servant,
A. Simpson.

Rory stared long and hard at the signature. Then he crossed to his little desk in the corner of his room and sharpened a quill pen to a fine point. Dipping it in the standish, he bent over the parchment and carefully and with delicate flourishes changed the "A" to an "H."

Then he changed the "i" of Simpson to an "a" and, sanding the letter, ran downstairs again.

He rummaged in an old desk of the late earl until he found a small anonymous-looking seal, and melting a blob of red sealing wax over the old broken seal, he stamped it firmly, and returned the letter to the tray in the hall.

His mother would get the letter, only it would appear to have come from Henrietta — a female that Rory remembered from the breakfast with intense dislike. He knew his mother disliked Miss Sampson also. She would ignore the letter, Rory judged, and assume that Miss Henrietta Sampson had run mad.

But this piece of mischief did not soothe his ruffled feelings as he had expected and he ambled aimlessly into the drawing room and stared out into the street.

How long it took for the days to begin in London!

Everyone who was anyone stayed up half the night and then spent most of the day in bed.

The Tsar of Russia and the King of Prussia were expected to make their state visits in June. Rory had enjoyed the parades and galas for the visit of the restored French monarch, Louis XVIII, and the celebrations for the Russian and Prussian monarchs promised to be grander still. That old hero Blücher, the Prussian commander, and Platov, the leader of the Russian Cossacks, were also due to arrive. Although his mother frowned on stories of war, Rory had picked up enough to admire and long to see these great allied commanders who had helped Wellington defeat Bonaparte . . . although Rory, like most Britishers, secretly thought the great Duke of Wellington could have done the job himself and with both hands tied behind his back.

There were also great Peace Celebrations planned for July.

But whatever was happening, whoever was arriving, you could be sure nothing would happen in the morning.

It was a miserable morning with a damp, wet fog pressing against the windowpanes.

Rory pricked up his ears as he heard the confused sound of voices coming along the street. Perhaps it was a raree man, come to display his bag of tricks on the doorstep. Rory polished the window with his sleeve and peered out into the mist.

Three rough-looking boys were walking along the street, carrying a sack between them and arguing loudly.

Rory continued to watch. There was nothing else to do anyway.

The boys stopped outside and one of them opened the sack and dragged out a wriggling striped cat. One of the others threw a rope over the lamppost and started to make a noose.

They were going to hang the cat.

Rory watched with interest.

Then the mist thinned and he saw the cat clearly. It was a big, shabby animal which had seen many back-alley fights. One ear was ragged and its mouth had once been torn, giving it a strange lopsided smile.

It had eyes as green as Lord Toby Freemantle's and it fought and clawed and struggled for its life.

But the boys were strong and they got the noose round the demented animal's neck.

Rory didn't know what happened to him that moment, but the next thing he knew he found himself out on the pavement, punching and clawing and biting like a fiend. The boys were much bigger than he but Rory took them by surprise. They dropped the cat, which crouched against the railings.

Rory placed his small figure in front of it and put up his fists. The boys had had time to recover from their shock and let out jeers of laughter at the sight of Rory in his frilly shirt, knee breeches and golden hair.

"Let's spoil 'is pwitty phiz," laughed the biggest and drove his fist into Rory's face — but fortunately Rory had been in a few scraps with the village boys and had learned every dirty trick in the book.

He proceeded to use every one he could. He managed to get in a few good jabs, but they were beginning to inflict more damage than they received. Blood was pouring from Rory's nose, his head was reeling, his clothes were torn.

He took a fierce pride in the fact that he was still somehow standing, that the cat was behind him, but he knew he could not last another minute. He had not even thought to cry for help.

The street door behind crashed open and Hamish hurtled out. Rory's assailants took to their heels and fled.

Rory wiped the blood from his face with his cuff and knelt down beside the cat. It lay very still, its eyes half closed. He put out a hand and stroked its great, awkward head.

"Now, laddie," began Hamish, "down to the kitchen wi' ye afore yer mither finds . . ."

"I want this animal taken care of," said Rory.

"Havers!" snapped Hamish. "Leave the dirty,

mangy beastie alone and get yerself inside at the double."

"I want him," he said slowly. "If you help me keep him, Hamish, I shall give you . . ." He broke off as the cat completely opened its eyes. There was something in that unwavering green stare that reminded Rory of Lord Toby.

He stood up and swung round, facing the butler with a quaint dignity. "I mean to say, Mr. Hamish, if you will help me to attend to this animal, I shall be extremely grateful to you. It is a kindness which I do not deserve but if you will not do it for me, at least do it for this unfortunate cat."

Hamish listened to this pompous little speech in amazement. The eyes that looked pleadingly up into his own seemed to be the eyes of a child for the first time.

"Och, well, laddie," muttered Hamish, feeling strangely embarrassed. "It'll do nae harm to tak' a look at the beast."

Hamish bent down and the cat lashed up at him. "There ye are!" said Hamish. "Disnae want tae be touched."

Rory bent down and lifted the heavy cat gently in his arms. It gave a faint miaow but lay still as he carried it into the house and down the stairs to the kitchens.

Hamish followed wonderingly behind. "Wheesht!" he shouted as two of the maidservants screamed at the sight of Rory's bloody face. "About your duties! Now, laddie, don't you think I'd better look at your ain injuries?"

"No," said Rory. "The cat first. He is bleeding a bit. See — on his side. Please may I have some warm water, Mr. Hamish?"

Rory had never said "please" to Hamish before, let alone called him "Mr." The butler poured hot water from the kettle on the fire into a metal bowl and added cold until it was right. Then he handed the boy the bowl and a pad of gauze.

"I suppose ye want a bit o' caviar for the beast?" said Hamish, watching as Rory cleaned the cat's fur with gentle hands.

"No," replied Rory, deaf to the sarcasm. "A little milk and some of that cold roast beef chopped up small will do. I shall arrange it."

"Ye certainly will," grumbled Hamish. "I'm no' acting butler tae a cat."

"See! He's smiling. He likes being clean," cried Rory.

Hamish looked cynically at the cat's evil, lopsided smile. "That's no a smile. That's whaur the beastie's tore his mouth."

"He smiled at me," insisted Rory. He moved to the table and hacked off a piece of roast beef and cut it into small cubes. Then he poured milk into a saucer and put it down on the floor beside the cat.

As the cat began to feebly lick the milk, Rory continued to clean him.

"When it has eaten something, I'll take it up to my room," said Rory dreamily.

The door opened before Hamish could answer and Scott, Morag's lady's maid, bustled in. She threw up her hands in horror when she saw Rory's face.

"I fell downstairs," said Rory quickly. "It is a nosebleed. Nothing more. Mr. Hamish is attending to me."

"Very well," said Scott. "I have a message for you from your mother. She has to make an urgent call to Miss Sampson and I am to go with her. She's in a fair taking. My lady says you are to wait until she returns. We will not be long."

Rory nodded, and when she had gone, he turned his attention back to the cat. He had forgotten all about the letter.

Morag could not remember being so angry in all her life. The day had started badly enough. Not only had Lord Arthur and his wife Phyllis come to town but old Cosmo, Laird of Glenaquer, had arrived as well, and both parties had sent messages to say they would be calling on her.

And then she had read that bombshell signed H. Sampson. Morag was unaware that she was jealous of Lord Toby's fiancée and therefore did not pause to wonder why a comparative stranger should write to her about Rory. She wanted to scratch Henrietta Sampson's eyes out. And now she had an excuse.

Miss Sampson was at home and pleased to receive Lady Murr. Or rather, she was socially pleased until Morag, hair and face flaming, thrust the letter under Henrietta's long nose and demanded an explanation.

"Someone obviously knows your son very well," said Henrietta coldly. "But I certainly did not write that letter. I do not concern myself with the family problems of every eccentric who graces the London Season. What on earth made you think I would do such a thing?"

"Jealousy," raged Morag, thereby proving that not even the kindest of heroines is immune from that very human failing of blaming someone else for her own faults.

"Jealous. Of you?" said Henrietta with an infuriating titter. "You know what I think, Lady Murr? *I* think you wrote that letter yourself so that you should have an excuse to call in this hurly-burly fashion and pick a quarrel."

Morag's back was to the door so she did not see Lord Toby quietly entering the room. But Henrietta did and so went on, "I am distressed that you should think such awful things of me, Lady Murr. But I forgive you." She clasped her hands and rolled her eyes up to heaven.

"I have come at an inopportune moment," began Lord Toby. Morag swung around. "Read this!" she cried, thrusting the letter at him. "And judge for yourself the depths of Miss Sampson's spite."

Lord Toby carefully scanned the letter. "Yes, I know Rory embellished the portrait," he said.

"What!" Morag felt as if the wind had indeed

been taken out of her sails. "Rory would never . . . wouldn't dream . . ."

"Rory does quite a lot of things of which you are obviously unaware," said Lord Toby, hoping nastily that he was making Morag feel as guilty as she had made him feel the day before. "You are the only person he hides it from. It is not my place to tell tales on the boy except to point out to you that the sooner you send him to school and find an outlet for that terrifying intelligence of his, the better."

"This letter . . ." pursued Morag faintly.

Lord Toby raised his quizzing glass and studied the signature. "I think you had better ask *Miss Simpson* about it. It seems to me as if this signature has been cleverly altered."

Morag stared at him in bewilderment. He thought she looked more adorable than ever. Henrietta, who felt that Lord Toby had not paid enough heed to the great insult offered to *her*, proceeded to stir up the troubled waters as hard as she could.

"You have been guilty of a great injustice," she said severely to Morag. "I am quite prepared, however, to accept your *humble* apology." Henrietta, having said that, primly folded her hands in her lap and cast down her eyes. A small saintly smile curved her lips.

Lord Toby suddenly felt overcome by a desire to shake his fiancée until her teeth rattled.

"No, I shall not apologize," snapped Morag. "I concede that you probably did not write the letter. But you are just the sort of nasty person who might have done."

And with this crashing piece of illogic, Morag stormed from Henrietta's drawing room and house.

Morag was very silent on the short journey home.

Rory was the one sweet and pure thing in her life. She would not believe ill of him; she could not. And if Miss Simpson had indeed written the letter then Miss Simpson would be dismissed.

After Morag had exclaimed over Rory's battered appearance and accepted his tale of falling downstairs, she sent for Miss Simpson.

Rory sat quietly in a corner of the room and watched Miss Simpson. His cat, whom he had christened "The Beastie," was lying upstairs on his bed. He stared reflectively at Miss Simpson and wondered if there were any way in which he could enlist her help. He felt sure his mother would not allow him to keep the cat. Morag did not approve of household pets. Cats were to be kept in the barn and dogs in the kennels.

"Miss Simpson," began Morag severely. "Did you send this letter? For if you did I shall have no other alternative but to dismiss you!"

Miss Simpson let out a little sigh. She might have known this would be the result. Morag was both kind and sensible — except when it came to Rory. He was her blind spot. In her mind's eye, Miss Simpson saw her shrewish sister-in-law and sighed again.

"Come, Miss Simpson," said Morag. "I am waiting!"

Still Miss Simpson remained curiously silent. The governess was looking at her mistress and thinking of how Morag had changed from the dreamy, immature girl she had tutored and had indeed become the Countess of Murr. Morag had had seven years of overseeing her estates and tenants, had become used to issuing commands, and expecting those commands to be obeyed. She was a mixture of a hot-headed beauty and an autocratic dowager. And at that moment, the autocratic dowager was uppermost.

Miss Simpson looked across at Rory, at the cause of all her ills. She took a deep breath and opened her mouth to speak.

"I wrote the letter, mama," said Rory.

"Rory!" Morag stared at him as if she could not believe her ears. Miss Simpson collapsed onto the nearest chair.

"I only did it because I wanted to get that terrible lady into trouble," said Rory bravely, feeling an almost heady sensation of excitement. Miss Simpson was staring at him in bewildered gratitude. This was almost as good as protecting the cat.

"I'm sorry, mama," said Rory brokenly, although he felt not in the least sad. "But she's such a nasty woman and she hates you. That made me mad."

"But I made such a fool of myself!" wailed Morag. "I accused her of all sorts of things." Another awful thought struck her. "Rory! Did you write that dreadful word on Lady Montclair's portrait? Lord Freemantle says you did!"

But Rory felt he had been truthful enough for one day. "No, mama," he cried. "I only put it in the letter. I don't even know what the word means! I don't know why Lord Freemantle should accuse me of such a thing. Oh, mama. I am truly sorry." Rory was indeed sorry. He hated to see his mother distressed. He hoped the championship of Miss Simpson was worth it.

"I'm afraid I must punish you," said Morag sadly, "so that you will never do such a thing again. I was to take you to Lady Jersey's children's ball. Now you will have to stay in your room for the rest of the day."

"Very good, mama," said Rory, hoping she would not change her mind. A whole day to play with his cat instead of going to some awful ball!

After he had left, Morag turned to Miss Simpson. "Pray forgive me," she said. "I am too hot-headed. I do not think I understand Rory at all! I would not have believed him capable of such a thing!"

Now was Miss Simpson's chance to enlighten her mistress but she remained carefully silent. The awful image of her sister-in-law began to fade.

"And now the very thought of entertaining the Laird of Glenaquer and Phyllis and Arthur is threatening to give me a nervous seizure. Cosmo will preach and my in-laws will sneer," sighed Morag.

"Perhaps," suggested Miss Simpson, inspired by relief, "you might arrange a dinner party and invite them as well. Much better to entertain them in a crowd."

"Splendid!" said Morag, her mind busy with the guest list. "I shall invite Miss Sampson by way of making amends — and Lord Freemantle of course." And I shall invite Lord Freddie, her treacherous mind plotted, and flirt with him the entire time and see how Lord Toby likes that!

Miss Simpson was kept busy the rest of the day with lists and errands. In the evening she was to accompany Morag to the Italian opera.

She did not have an opportunity to go to Rory's room until very late. She gently pushed open his bedroom door. He was fast asleep, his arm flung over a dark shape on the bed. Miss Simpson crept closer. An evil-looking cat with a lopsided smile looked lazily up at her. She stood contemplating the cat for some time. So that was the reason Rory had taken the blame. He had found something other than his mother to love. She knew that Morag could not know of the existence of the cat.

Miss Simpson went out and closed the door. Though Rory obviously had had an ulterior motive in taking the blame for the letter, she was, nonetheless, still very grateful to him. Which was just as well.

Since she wasn't going to enjoy this novel feeling for long.

Chapter Ten

The day of Morag's dinner party finally arrived — although at times she thought it never would. She determinedly put down her feelings of anticipation to all the natural apprehension of a hostess giving her first London party. And anytime her treacherous thoughts flew to Lord Toby she crushed them down. She had made a most awful fool of herself over that letter. He must have taken her in dislike. He would not come. It did not matter whether he did.

But Lord Toby and Miss Henrietta Sampson were both delighted to attend. Lord Toby because he wanted to show Morag how little he really cared for her, and Henrietta, to crow over her rival.

Cosmo, the laird, and Lord Arthur and Lady Phyllis were also to be there. Lord Freddie Rotherwood had gleefully accepted.

Alistair Tillary and Harvey Wrexford had both been honored with invitations and, because she felt she must have some more female company, Morag had invited an elderly dowager, Lady Cynthia Wells, famous for her acid tongue and quite capable of keeping Cosmo in order, and the pretty Charrington sisters, Alice and Beth.

Alice and Beth Charrington were lively young ladies of boundless frivolity and good nature and could be depended on to talk through any awkward social silence. Alice was nineteen and Beth, twenty. They had pretty, rosy faces and masses of brown ringlets which they tossed up and down like nervous ponies.

Morag had vowed to treat Henrietta with extra-special courtesy and Lord Toby with the barest of civility. Before the guests were due to arrive, she studied her reflection anxiously in the long looking glass. She was wearing one of her favorite tunic dresses, of light green silk worn over a flimsy lingerie dress of finest muslin with no less than three deep flounces at the hem.

A heavy necklace of emeralds was clasped round her neck. A small emerald and gold tiara blazed on her fiery curls. She hoped Cosmo would not recognize the Murr emeralds in their new setting. The laird did not appear to like change, and Morag sometimes thought he seemed to consider the Murr estates his own. She had lately learned that the earl's first wife had been a distant relation of Cosmo's and perhaps the laird felt that that gave him some right to poke his nose into her affairs. However, Morag reflected, the late Lady Murr had died years and years before her own marriage to the earl, the earl had never mentioned her and there was no portrait of her in the castle so she could not be considered a strong influence. She had evidently been as young as Morag when she had married the earl and had survived only a year of marriage.

Morag picked up an ivory and silk fan and walked downstairs to inspect the drawing room and dining room.

At first everything appeared to be perfect. The dining table was all set with crystal, silver, china and two tablecloths, the top one to be removed before the pudding. The drawing room was fragrant with fresh flowers and a small fire crackled on the hearth, for the evening was unseasonably cold.

Then she stared at the elegant backless sofa with its green and striped gold bolsters, and frowned. Long scratches were scored into the gilt-painted wood.

She rang the bell and, when Hamish appeared, silently pointed to the scratches. Hamish hesitated. He was oddly reluctant to explain the cat. "I would ask Master Rory," he said at last.

"Rory?" Morag flushed. For some reason she remembered Lord Toby saying that Rory had embellished Lady Montclair's picture. But he had been innocent of that. Hadn't he? "Send Rory to me," she said quietly.

She paced up and down until the door of the drawing room opened and Rory sidled in, a picture in his party dress of blue velvet knee breeches, matching waistcoat, square-cut jacket and buckled shoes.

"How came these scratches on the sofa?" asked Morag.

The boy hesitated. Then he put his hands behind his back, a gesture preliminary to lying which Hamish would have instantly recognized. "I do not know, mama," he said, turning a limpid gaze on her.

"Are you quite sure?" asked Morag, for the first time not immediately accepting his word.

"You doubt my word?" said Rory, widening his eyes.

"Do not answer one question with another," said Morag severely. "I want you to give me your solemn word of honor that you have no idea how these scratches came about."

"I give you my solemn word of honor," said Rory, putting his hand over his heart.

"Very well then," sighed Morag. "I must question the maid in the morning. You may stay with me, Rory. Our guests are due to arrive."

Rory experienced a slight qualm of unease. He had left The Beastie asleep on his bed but he had also left the door to his bedroom open. He could only hope that The Beastie remained asleep until he had a chance to escape upstairs.

Lady Phyllis and Lord Arthur were the first to arrive. Phyllis's eyes flicked round the room and fastened enviously on Morag's gown and jewels. A great deal of money and an instinctive flair for dress had put Morag well beyond Phyllis's barbs. The Charrington sisters arrived next, giggling and chattering, followed by Alistair and Harvey. Then came Lady Cynthia Wells, resplendent in black bombazine and Whitby jet, looking, with her pale-yellow leathery skin, for all the world like some kind of exotic lizard. Cosmo arrived and addressed his courtesies to Morag while his eyes fastened on the emeralds. "I would ha' expected tae see ye wearin' caps," he began. "Aye, Morag, we're all gettin' on in years and we should dress as befits oor station."

"That is precisely what I have done," said Morag sweetly.

Cosmo opened his mouth to reply but Morag had moved away to greet Lord Toby and Henrietta.

Morag was glad to escape. In appearance, Cosmo looked like a sort of blurred version of her former husband.

Her heart hammering against her ribs, Morag addressed various innocuous pleasantries to Henrietta, while all the time she was painfully aware of every inch of Toby Freemantle.

He was wearing a dark blue evening coat which seemed moulded to his figure. His handsome, rather austere face rose above the snowy folds of an impeccable cravat. His knee breeches and clocked stockings showed his muscular legs to perfection.

Lord Freddie Rotherwood breezed in and Morag went forward and greeted him very warmly indeed, her blue eyes glinting sideways to see how Lord Toby was taking it.

He was looking down fondly at his fiancée. He laughed, said something and patted her hand. Morag blushed from sheer excess of emotion and Lord Freddie's hopes of marrying this Scottish heiress rose by leaps and bounds.

Toby has really no interest in me — no respectable interest that is, thought Morag. He only wants to have an affair with me. But he is in love with Henrietta. And I hate her with all my heart.

"How terribly funny, Lord Freddie," she said out loud, giving a trill of laughter although she had not heard a word he had said. But Freddie usually told jokes and so she assumed it safe to laugh. And Freddie, who had been telling her that his favorite aunt had died only the day before, stared at her with some surprise.

Rory began to edge from the room. Miss Simpson had joined the party, making it complete. He wanted to talk to Lord Toby, but he simply had to see that The Beastie had stayed in his room.

"Well, young man. What have you to say for yourself?" It was Cosmo, Laird of Glenequer, and he had caught Rory by the lapel of his jacket. Rory wondered why Cosmo bothered to single him out since the laird's eyes always held that strange contempt that he saw mirrored in the eyes of Mrs. Tallant and Hamish.

"I'm very well," began Rory. Then he heard loud feminine screams and he knew the game was up.

The screams stopped and there was silence. The crowd parted, the ladies holding back their skirts as a huge, mangy tabby with a lopsided grin strolled insolently through the room, went straight to the sofa and proceeded to sharpen its claws.

Unfortunately for Rory, Hamish had left the room to supervise another tray of refreshments and the new footman, Gerald, was handing round the glasses.

"Take that thing out of here," cried Morag, "and put it in the gutter where it belongs."

Rory stayed quiet. He would simply creep out into the street and fetch the cat back.

But Gerald said cheerfully, "That's my lord's cat, my lady."

"My lord? Which lord?" demanded Morag.

"Master Rory," said Gerald.

"Rory!" cried Morag. "Is this true?"

Rory held his arms wide in a gesture that was meant to be appealing, and to his horror, The Beastie jumped right into his open arms, affectionately lolled its great misshapen head over his shoulder and went to sleep.

"Come with me, Rory," said Morag quietly and led the way from the room.

Henrietta gleefully watched them go. Lord Toby watched also, but he was not sharing his fiancée's enjoyment.

Morag led the way into a small study at the back of the house.

"Now, Rory," she said. "You lied to me. What I would like to know is — how many times have you lied in the past?"

"Many times," drawled a familiar voice from

the doorway. Lord Toby Freemantle stood, leaning against the door jamb, his green eyes, so like the cat's, fastened on Rory.

"This is not your affair, my lord," began Morag hotly. But Lord Toby paid her no heed, and strolled into the room.

"I do not know why I champion this brat," he said, flicking Rory's chin with a careless finger and smiling down at the boy, who still clutched the large and heavy cat to his bosom. "Perhaps because I recognize an intelligent mind going to waste. Don't be too hard on the boy, Morag. He needs occupation. He should be allowed to run and play and hunt and shoot like other boys of his age. You protect him too much and that is why he lies to you — apart from thc fact he is a naturally horrible brat," he said turning and smiling at her in such a way that she felt breathless.

"First things first," said Morag, trying to regain control of the situation. "That cat goes!"

"No!" cried Rory. "He — he's mine. I saved his life. I won him in a fight. I lied, I didn't fall down the stairs that day. But if I had told you then, you would have worried and you wouldn't have let me keep The Beastie."

"More lies!" said Morag bitterly.

"Are you so shocked because your child is normal?" said Lord Toby, looking at her coolly. He turned back to Rory. "Tell me about the fight."

And Rory, eyes shining, began to tell of the

saving of The Beastie. At first, he cast little nervous glances at Morag's tight face but the flattering attention of Lord Toby made him warm to his story.

"Bravely done," said Lord Toby, after he had heard him out. "I would not have thought you capable of caring for anything other than yourself or your mother. Let him have this cat, Morag. The dreadful animal might be the making of him." He scratched The Beastie's heavy head and the cat stretched lazily.

"But all those lies!" cried Morag.

"I think if you let him keep the cat and find him a tutor, he will not lie to you again. Will you?"

Rory hesitated. "Would a tutor teach me all those things you said . . . st-steamships and insects and . . . how the stars move and oh . . . everything?" he asked, stammering in his excitement.

"If your mother will let me find you a tutor, he shall teach you all these things. He will even teach you to box."

Rory turned his eyes on Morag. She had never seen him look so intense. "I swear, mother," said Rory. "I'll never tell another lie. I really promise."

"Let me think about it," said Morag faintly. "Go to your room and take that . . . animal with you."

Rory walked out, cradling the cat.

There was a heavy silence.

Then Lord Toby shut the study door and

turned to face Morag. Her head was whirling with a mixture of emotions. It seemed unfair that, considering the child was not her own, she should suffer all the pangs of maternal guilt and this fit of the oh-where-did-I-go-wrongs. Also, no man should be endowed with such a heavy air of sensuality as Lord Toby Freemantle. The room felt hot and suffocating. She rose to her feet and went across and jerked open the windows which led from the study onto the terrace at the back of the house.

A cold, white fog rolled in, but, oblivious to the weather, Morag walked out onto the terrace and clutched the stone balustrade.

"You will let me choose a tutor for the boy?" came Toby's voice from behind her.

She nodded her head dumbly.

He hesitated. Henrietta would be wondering where he was. But her shoulders were very white and little beads of mist gleamed like diamonds in the tendrils of her hair.

"I have done the very best I could," Morag was saying in a low voice. "If Rory had been . . ." She fell silent and he wondered what it was she had been going to say. The logical end to the sentence was "had been my own," but that was ridiculous.

"He needs a father," he said, coming to stand close behind her.

"Is he so very bad?" she asked, looking out to the mist-enshrouded garden.

"I don't know the full extent of Rory's iniquities," he teased, then added in a more serious tone, "I will do what I can to help, Morag."

She turned then and looked up at him. He looked down at the love and bewilderment in her eyes.

He was being offered the world but he could not stretch out his arms and take it. Obedience to the social conventions was built into every fiber of his body. He made a half move to take her in his arms and then said stiffly, "We must join the guests."

The light went out of Morag's eyes. He held out his arm. She put her arm in his and then, just for a moment, rested her head against his shoulder. Then she said lightly, "You have given me a new purpose in life — finding a father for Rory. Perhaps I should marry Freddie. That might answer."

"You are joking," he said flatly as they walked from the room.

"No," she replied, stopping before the doors of the drawing room and looking up at him. "It might answer all my problems."

She left him to join Lord Freddie and he found himself claimed by Henrietta.

Hamish announced dinner and Morag and Lord Freddie led the way into the dining room. Beth Charrington saw a glass of milk standing on the side table in the hall and giggled, "You should have that glass of milk *chained* to the table, dear Lady Murr. So hard to get now what with the celebrations and bands and fireworks in

Green Park frightening the cows so much that they will not give any more milk!"

Morag turned in the doorway of the dining room. "Oh, that is Rory's milk," she said. "Hamish, see that it is taken up to him."

"I will take it," said Miss Simpson. She felt obliged to thank Rory for covering up for her over the matter of the letter and she had been unable to see him alone. Perhaps if she did not, he would change his mind and tell Morag the truth.

"There is really no need . . ." began Morag, but Miss Simpson was already on her way upstairs.

Rory was sitting up in his bed reading. The Beastie was lying at his feet. He looked up as Miss Simpson came in, bearing the glass of milk.

"I don't want it," he said crossly. "Give it to The Beastie."

"If you mean that creature of yours, no, I will not," said Miss Simpson. "Milk is too scarce these days to waste on a cat."

"Nothing is too good for my cat," said Rory in a pompous little voice.

Miss Simpson forgot that she owed her existence in the household to the cat. She forgot her gratitude to Rory.

"He is a horrible, disgusting cat — only fit for back alleys and *NOT* for a gentleman's house. I shall tell your mama you did not drink your milk."

"You want it! *You* have it," said Rory crossly, "and shut the door and take a good look at it from the other side."

163

Chapter Eleven

Lord Toby Freemantle lay in bed on the morning after Morag's dinner party and tried to think the very worst of his hostess.

She was extremely silly when it came to that son of hers. Her treatment of him went against everything he knew of her. Had it not been for Rory, he would have judged her an eminently sensible woman. She had lost that shy, bewildered look of the Scottish days. Perhaps it had all been an act. She had had the managing of a vast fortune for the past seven years and it showed in her poise and slightly autocratic manner. And it was not just her wealth that gave Morag her sophistication of dress, for he had known many heiresses who dressed very badly indeed. Where had Morag come by it?

He would not allow the truth — that Morag had taken to the fripperies and vagaries of fashionable London like a duck to water and was blessed with natural good taste.

He brooded instead on the possible existence of some dashing Scottish lover. She was hot-blooded and passionate. He could not believe in his darker moments that she had remained faithful to the earl's memory.

Could he rid himself of Henrietta? Did he really dislike her as much as he thought he did, or was his aversion caused by this impossible yearning for Morag?

He was aroused from his uneasy meditations by a soft scratching at the door. In answer to his abrupt "Enter!" his footman sidled in, looking coy.

"There is a lady below to see my lord. She would not give her name."

Lord Toby stared at the man coldly. "I do not receive women who arrive unannounced. Does she have a maid with her?"

"No, my lord."

"Then send her packing."

The footman hesitated. "She is very grandly dressed, my lord. And ever so high in her manner."

Lord Toby looked at him thoughtfully. "Does she have red hair?"

"Very red, my lord."

"Show her up to my sitting room. And take that smirk from your face. No news of the visit is to reach the kitchens or the street. Understand?"

"Yes, my lord."

Lord Toby sprang from his bed and ran his hand anxiously over the stubble on his chin. He would not have time to be barbered. He could ask Morag to wait — if it were she — but she might take fright and leave.

He pulled on his breeches and cambric shirt,

his morocco slippers and a chintz dressing gown and pushed open the door of his private sitting room which adjoined his bedroom.

It was indeed Morag, looking very white and shaken. "I did not know what else to do," she said and he walked forward and took her hands in his. "Oh, Toby, I am so frightened."

He thought his name on her lips sounded like music. He drew her to a small sofa and still holding her hands said quietly, "Tell me. I will do all I can to help."

"It's Miss Simpson," she gasped. "She's dead. Poisoned! And the poison was in the milk meant for Rory. He would not drink it and she drank it herself. And now she's dead! And I only came to London to take Rory out of danger!" Her eyes were wide with apprehension as her tale tumbled forth.

"Has there been a previous attempt?"

Morag nodded weakly. She told him of the shot and then of the attempted kidnapping.

"So I began to wonder whether Lord Arthur had any designs on Rory's life because he is always short of money and would inherit if anything happened to Rory. And then there's Cosmo. He dislikes Rory because Rory is not the earl's natural son . . ."

She stopped and put a shaking hand to her lips, her face pale. "Oh, I should not have told you."

"Who is Rory's mother?" he demanded, his eyes fixed intently on her face.

"Fionna, a kitchenmaid," she whispered. "My — my husband asked me to take the child as my own."

"What of this Fionna?"

"Dead — died in childbirth." And Morag told him of the day when Rory had been born in a field under the hawthorn tree.

"And where are this girl's parents?"

"They died of typhoid several years before her own death."

"But my dear girl," expostulated Toby. "Your husband asked a great deal of you. I wonder you agreed."

"It was after you left," said Morag dully. "He knew about you and I — what little there was to know. I felt I ought to try to make amends — for sinning in desire, if not in action."

"And did you?"

"What?"

"Desire it?"

"I suppose so," whispered Morag.

He fought down a rising feeling of elation and said quietly, "Tell me about Miss Simpson. Did you call the authorities?"

"Oh, yes," said Morag. "As soon as I found out. I have not even been to bed. An officer from the Bow Street Horse Patrol was sent for. He said Miss Simpson had probably committed suicide because he said, 'These old maids do get twitty.' " Her lower lip trembled slightly.

"The Robin Redbreasts are not usually so dense."

"And he didn't know what the poison was. He said maybe the milk was bad but, oh, her face, all purple and contorted!"

Morag buried her face in her hands.

"Don't cry. Please don't cry," he said, pulling her into his arms. "I will take care of you. Listen to me! There is a retired boxer I know of. A very reliable and honest man. You will employ him as the boy's tutor. He may not be able to do much for Rory in the way of book-learning but he will protect him and stay with him night and day." He looked down at her. "Why did you come to me?" he could not help asking. "Did you not think of Lord Rotherwood?"

Morag's voice was muffled against his chest. "I-I felt that you cared for Rory. Oh, who can be trying to kill him?"

Any one of the top ten thousand, thought Lord Toby, thinking of Rory's talents for blackmail and mischief. But he did not say so aloud.

She was wearing a ridiculous, frivolous bonnet with an enormous poke brim. He gently untied the ribbons and took it off. Then he pulled out a pocket handkerchief and, raising her chin, gently dried her tears.

Morag became aware for the first time of the intimacy of their situation. He look heartbreakingly handsome, with his hair disheveled and his chin unshaven.

"And what of your desires?" he asked.

Her eyes flew up to meet his and then dropped.

"You have no right to ask me such a thing," she said. She put her hands against his chest to push him away.

"Damn Henrietta!" he said thickly and jerked her into his arms.

But Toby, for all his sophistication and address, could still make the callowest of errors. He should have said he loved her.

For although Morag returned his kisses with passion, she knew that Lord Toby considered her only good enough for idle dalliance — certainly not respectable enough to marry.

But the second mistake Lord Toby made was a forgivable one — for how on earth was he to know that the widow he held in his arms was a virgin? And so when he bent his head and began to cover her neck and breast with impassioned kisses, she let out a cry of outrage and boxed his ears.

"I must go," panted Morag, seizing her bonnet and tying it at an awkward angle over her red curls.

He stood looking at her strangely. "I do not understand you," he said.

"Then you have more hair than wit," snapped Morag, her cheeks flushed and her eyes sparkling. "You are not going to philander with me while your heart and your hand belong elsewhere!"

"Morag!" he cried.

But she ran swiftly from the room, anger lending her feet wings. He hesitated a moment and then pursued her. But by the time he reached the hall, the street door had slammed in his face and he could hardly run after her carriage in his slippers.

For Morag it was the beginning of a nightmarish day. She hurtled into the hallway of her town house in Albemarle Street, to receive the unwelcome news that Cosmo, Laird of Glenaquer, was waiting for her in the drawing room.

"Hamish, is Rory well?"

"Very well, my leddy," said Hamish. "I have kept Rory and that cat of his with me in the kitchens. He likes playing there and I thought it safer. My leddy, I have received a most unusual message frae Mrs. Tallant . . ."

"Not now, Hamish," said Morag, opening the door of the drawing room.

Cosmo rose to his feet and made her a creaky bow. He was a heavyset man attired in frock coat and knee breeches. It was perhaps his nut-brown wig and slightly protruding eyes which reminded Morag so much of her late husband.

"This is a sad business," said the laird. "It is too much for a young lass like yersel tae handle alone. I would hae spoken sooner but I held back in memory of old Roderick. What I am aboot tae say will gratify ye and maybe lift a bit o' the gloom frae this house o' mourning."

As Morag stared at him wonderingly, he fell clumsily to one knee. "My darlin'," he said in a sonorous voice, "you have the great honor to receive my proposal of marriage."

"No!" cried Morag, putting her hands to her hot cheeks. "I mean, I am very flattered. But — but I cannot marry anyone."

Cosmo rose slowly and clumsily to his feet, his face becoming quite red with anger. "Oho! So that's the way of it. Ye've got Roderick's money by a trick, and that's made ye too high and mighty for auld Cosmo. Well, let me tell ye this. What think you an I told the world that the young Earl o' Murr is a bastard got by a kitchen maid?"

"You could not be so cruel!" said Morag.

"Think aboot it," said Cosmo, brushing down his coat. "I'll be back tomorrow for yer answer. Either ye wed me, lass, or the fashionable world will hear an odd tale of that lad's ancestry."

He marched from the room and Morag sat down on a chair and buried her face in her hands.

"Lord Frederick Rotherwood," intoned Hamish gloomily from the door.

"Oh, no! I cannot see him. I am quite overset," began Morag but Freddie had already bounced into the room.

"What on earth is the matter?" he questioned, his boyish face looking concerned. "I did not think you would be so upset over Miss Simpson," he said, remembering her mirth at the news of his aunt's demise. "Although the circumstances of her death . . ."

"It's not that," wailed Morag, too upset to guard her tongue. "It's Cosmo!"

"You mean that old Scot I met at dinner. What's he to do with it?"

"He is trying to make me marry him."

"What! He cannot do that. This isn't the Middle Ages."

"It may as well be," said Morag bitterly. Realizing she should be silent, but won over by Freddie's open and sympathetic look. "He — he knows something about . . . about me and if I do not marry him, he will tell all of London and I will be ruined!" Morag burst out crying.

He knelt down in front of her and took her hands in his own. "Look," he said awkwardly. "Was going to ask you to marry me but it's not the right time. Will you leave things to me? I'll fix Cosmo. Whatever your dark secret is, it won't trouble me in the slightest. Come now! Dry your eyes and let old Freddie look after you."

Morag give him a weak smile and he leaned forward and kissed her on the cheek.

And that interesting tableau was viewed in silence by Lord Toby Freemantle, Miss Henrietta Sampson, and Lord and Lady Fleming who had all arrived on Morag's doorstep at the one time and had been ushered into the drawing room by the second footman, Hamish having been called to the kitchens.

Lord and Lady Fleming looked sour, Henrietta looked delighted and Lord Toby Freemantle felt as if the bottom had dropped out of his world.

"May we wish you happy?" said Henrietta coyly.

172

"Not yet," said Freddie cheerfully. "But any day now."

Morag made a feeble little motion with her hand. She wanted to protest. She wanted them all to go away. But the second footman was already bringing in a tray of refreshments and everyone sat around, prepared to wait the others out. Freddie, because he felt Morag had not quite taken in that he had asked her, in a way, to marry him; Henrietta to make quite sure that Morag had no further interest in Toby; Lord and Lady Fleming, to borrow money; and Lord Toby to tell her he loved her, which was something he realized he had forgotten to do.

Morag pulled herself together and dispensed tea to Henrietta and Lady Phyllis while the gentlemen fortified themselves from the decanters.

All murmured suitable things about the late Miss Simpson. Poor Miss Simpson! Not one person in the room really missed her at all.

Rory bounced in, his blond curls flying, and The Beastie lurching after him like a dog at his heels.

"Mama!" he cried. "There is some old wood in the garden and you know we never use the garden and Hamish says if I am good he will give me a hammer and nails to build a house for The Beastie. May I? Please say 'yes.' "

"Now Rory," said Morag severely, "you know I don't want you to play with nasty things like nails. You could do yourself an injury." But something drew Morag's eyes away from Rory and she met the green enigmatic stare of Lord Toby.

"On second thought," she said rapidly, "I suppose it could do no harm. You will be careful, darling, won't you?"

"Oh, *yes*," said Rory. He made an excellent bow to the company, seeming to be aware of them for the first time.

Freddie gave him a smile. He had better learn to like this horrible child. He was to be Rory's stepfather, after all.

"Are you looking forward to the Peace Celebrations?" he asked in what he hoped was a paternal manner.

"Yes, very much," said Rory, now fretting to get away. "I suppose we are quite friends with France now. I even heard some man at Lady Montclair's party say he was a loyal subject of Napoleon Bonaparte, but I can't remember who."

The visitors all stared at Rory with expressions that varied from surprise to concern.

"Probably one of those Frog actors Lady Montclair had to entertain her guests," drawled Lord Arthur.

"Oh, no, he wasn't French," said Rory blithely. "There was a French fellow with him. Please can I go now, mama?"

Morag nodded and Rory scooped his cat up into his arms and scampered out. There was a little silence.

"He must have imagined the whole thing," said Henrietta. "Children are so imaginative."

"Of course," said Lord Freddie, his face clearing.

They all began to talk about the Peace Celebrations and then to turn over the black subject of Miss Simpson's death. Lord and Lady Fleming and Henrietta were convinced the milk had been bad. Lord Freddie was sure Miss Simpson had added too much sleeping draught to it. Only Lord Toby remained silent, his green eyes fastened on Morag's face.

If only Henrietta would go away, he thought. He had not meant to upset Morag so much. She looked so pale and shaken that he began to feel worried. Let Henrietta sue him for breach of promise! He realized he could never look at another woman again. But perhaps he was too late — had she already accepted Freddie?

It was useless to wait here. He would be better employed in finding that tutor for Rory. He could return and question the boy about that conversation he had overheard at Lady Montclair's later.

Henrietta insisted on leaving with him. Then Freddie left, after pressing Morag's hand warmly.

The Flemings remained. From long experience, Morag knew exactly what they wanted and silently wrote Lord Arthur a note to take to her bank before he could begin his usual convolvulated dunning.

Now at last she was alone. Just a few minutes alone to try to sort out her burning thoughts.

"My leddy."

"What is it, Hamish? I am in no mood to cope with household problems."

"This concerns Rory," said Hamish grimly.

Morag poured herself a stiff measure of brandy from the decanter. "Go on, Hamish."

"I've had a letter from Mrs. Tallant. She says that the man who fired the bullet at Rory has been caught."

"Who was it?" cried Morag, draining her brandy in one gulp and choking slightly as the fiery liquid caught at the back of her throat.

"It was a poacher, Jamie Sutherland, a wild lad from the village. He was bragging about it when he was in his cups doon at the local ale house. Mr. Baillie, the steward, had him arrested. Sutherland said he didnae mean any harm. He only meant to give Rory a fright."

Hamish hesitated. "It seems that Rory was in the habit o' sneakin' oot o' the castle when we was all abed. Mr. Baillie charged him wi' trying to kidnap the boy as well but Sutherland says it sounded like one o' Rory's tales."

"Get Rory here immediately."

Rory came scampering in and then stopped at the sight of the set look on Morag's face.

"Rory," she said. "Mr. Baillie has found the boy who shot at you. It was Jamie Sutherland."

"Oh, him," said Rory with great indifference. "He was always bragging about what a great shot he was and he got angry when I laughed at him and said that one day he would part my curls with a bullet."

"And what about the kidnapping?" demanded Morag in a low voice. "Tell me the truth, Rory, or I shall . . . I shall . . . take that cat away from you."

Rory turned white. "No! You wouldn't be so cruel."

He stared anxiously at Morag's face. He had never seen her look so stern.

"Very well," he said sulkily. "I made it up. I'd gone to climb my favorite tree and I got stuck at the top. I knew if I told you, I'd never be able to get out again — don't look like that, mama! I just wanted to play like the other boys."

"You could have saved me a great deal of worry by telling the truth," said Morag, feeling suddenly tired. "Leave us, Rory. I shall speak to you later."

When the boy had trailed out, she turned to Hamish. "Then it appears as if Miss Simpson's death was an accident?"

"It certainly seems so, my leddy," said Hamish. "You should see her room. She had aboot every patent medicine in the land in her closet and some o' thae concoctions go bad, I've heard. Och, the auld girl did it tae herself, mark my words."

Morag smiled. "It seems I have got myself in a state over nothing." Then she remembered Cosmo's threat and her face clouded over. "Sit down, Hamish," she said. "I have more bad news for you."

She told him of Cosmo's threat and Hamish

listened intently.

"He'd no do it," said Hamish when he had heard her out. "He always was a terrible coward was the laird. He was always threatenin' folks but he'd no do it. I'll hae a wee word in his ear. He'll no trouble you again."

"Oh, Hamish," sighed Morag, "what would I do without you. There is one last thing. Lord Freemantle was to send a retired pugilist to masquerade as Rory's tutor and be a sort of watchdog. I shall send you round to Lord Freemantle with a note saying that we do not need this individual, unless," she laughed, "Rory has been unearthing French spies."

She told Hamish of the conversation Rory had overheard.

Blast the boy! thought Hamish. He did not want to further upset his mistress by pointing out that what Rory had overheard could be very serious indeed.

Instead he said, "I think you should let this boxer fellow come along just the same. It would do the boy the world o' good tae have some rough company. He's been treated a bit too much like a lassie, if ye'll forgive my speaking so plain, my leddy."

"Yes, you are right," sighed Morag. "Let us have him then." She should put Lord Toby Freemantle firmly out of her mind. His intentions were strictly dishonorable and she should have nothing more to do with him.

But her treacherous emotions at war with

her brain cried out for an excuse to see him again.

"Now, my leddy!" said Hamish, making as if to rise, "is there anything else?"

"No, Hamish. Oh, dear *yes*. Lord Rotherwood wishes to marry me and I told him about Cosmo."

"Lord save us! Ye never told him about Rory?"

"No, I simply said that Cosmo had some hold over me."

Hamish shook his head. "Whit a day," he said. "Tak' my advice and forget about the whole thing. It'll work itself out, never fear. Leave it to Hamish."

Morag smiled at him gratefully, reflecting there was a lot to be said for having Scottish servants. The polite world would be shocked to the core had they known she was in the habit of consulting her butler on every affair. The fact that she called him by his first name had raised enough eyebrows.

"You are right, Hamish," she said wearily. "Goodness knows, nothing else can happen today!"

Cosmo, Laird of Glenaquer, was feeling very pleased with himself. Morag's fortune added to his own would make him one of the richest men in Scotland. Of course, he would not have dreamed of telling anyone anything about Rory. He had given the earl his word and, for all his weakness, the laird was a man of honor when it came to other men. But women were different. They were soft, useless things who needed a firm hand. He was still a fine figure of a man and Morag would be better off with someone like himself than a callow Englishman.

He stopped in Pall Mall to watch the band of the Coldstream Guards with its giant negroes striking their cymbals with high, rhythmic blows. It was a splendid sound. Those black fellows must be almost seven feet tall! Like a schoolboy, he waited for the next great crash of the cymbals. The negroes raised their massive arms, the great cymbals glittering in a pale watery sunlight. Crash!

It was a mighty sound. So mighty that no one in the crowd heard the report of the bullet which took Cosmo between the shoulders and passed him on to the other world.

"Oh, these drunks!" cried a lady in a high-waisted muslin dress as Cosmo fell at her feet. "They shouldn't ought to be allowed, now should they?"

Cosmo lay there until the band marched away. He lay while an urchin picked his pockets. He lay there until the new gas lamps flared bravely above him and the watch, turning him over with a heavy foot, saw the bullet hole in his back.

Chapter Twelve

The only bright spot in the following weeks in Morag's gloomy life was the presence of Joseph Service, Rory's watchdog.

Although she felt Rory no longer needed to be guarded, nonetheless she felt relieved to know what Rory was doing every minute of the night and day. Mr. Service and Rory had become firm friends and they made an odd couple, the rough, lumbering boxer with his bald head and bandy legs and the beautiful fair-haired child.

He may not have been much of a tutor when it came to book-learning, but Mr. Service was a fund of information of the kind to delight a small boy — prize fights, poaching, hunting, fishing and the army.

Lord Toby had only called once and had seemed cold and distant. His sole interest appeared to be in finding out the name of the man that Rory had overheard talking at Lady Montclair's party. In fact, Lord Toby was having difficulty with the idea of telling Henrietta he had made a mistake. He was still very much bound by the conventions and Henrietta had more than once let fall laughing little remarks about breach of promise.

Miss Simpson had been duly buried and Cosmo's body had been packed in ice and sent north to rest in the churchyard on his estate. Morag was torn between relief that Cosmo was no longer around to plague her and a lurking feeling of danger. It had all been so opportune! The thick-headed officer from the Horse Patrol had pointed out that Cosmo had been killed and robbed, an everyday happening. Usually gentlemen of Cosmo's rank did not parade the streets without some sort of protection. He implied that Lady Murr had an overworked imagination.

Lord Freddie could not have done such a thing. But Hamish! Hamish was fanatically loyal. And underneath all her worries lay the perpetual nagging ache of longing for Lord Toby.

Freddie was assiduous in his attentions. He had not repeated his offer of marriage but seemed to take it for granted that they had an understanding. Morag wondered wearily whether to accept him or not. He was friendly and cheerful and undemanding company. *He* would not become engaged to one lady and philander with another. Only look how Toby had tried to seduce her when she was a married woman! He had no morals. Henrietta was welcome to him. On and on ran her troubled thoughts.

Because of the deaths of Miss Simpson and Cosmo, she had refused all social invitations. But she soon began to feel lonely. Rory preferred the company of Mr. Service to her own and she could not help feeling slightly jealous.

Freddie called as usual to try to persuade her to go for a drive with him and this time she found herself accepting.

Morag had to admit she felt much better as Lord Freddie tooled his smart curricle through the gates of Hyde Park. All the fashionables had turned out in the bright sunshine, dresses fluttering, carriages glistening in the hot, breezy, sunny day.

She was wearing a blue muslin gown the color of her eyes and gold Roman sandals on her feet. She unfurled her parasol since the sun was hot and her pretty hat was merely a puff of blond straw and ribbons.

Lord Freddie was pointing out all the Notables. He chattered at a great rate, never seeming to expect a reply other than "yes," "no" or "really" and Morag was content to listen to him. Then she became aware that he was saying, "Hey, there's Freemantle and Miss Sampson!" Lord Toby neatly edged his carriage next to Lord Freddie's and raised his hat. Henrietta gave a stiff little bow.

"Has Rory discovered the identity of the Bonapartiste?" asked Lord Toby, his hard eyes fixed on Morag's pale face.

"No," said Morag. "He probably made it up. I am afraid Rory invents things."

"Yes," tittered Henrietta. "He *does* tell lies, doesn't he? But I gather he will soon have a new papa." She smiled coyly at Lord Freddie who grinned back.

"Right you are," said Freddie cheerfully. "Don't worry. I'll send the little blighter to school." Morag stared at him in amazement and opened her mouth to say something, but Freddie had already touched his hat and flicked the reins and was moving rapidly away. "Cattle are fresh," he said by way of explanation. "Can't keep 'em standing."

"You should not have said that," said Morag. "I-I did not say I would marry you, Freddie."

"Oh, you will," he said in his usual cheery way. "Not hankering after anyone else, are you?"

Morag did not reply and he took her silence for assent. "Well, there you are. Faint heart never won fair lady, and I'll get you to the altar yet. Don't worry. I ain't asking you to make up your mind yet."

"But you should not have taken it upon yourself to speak so freely in front of . . . in front of Miss Sampson," protested Morag.

"I did, didn't I?" said Freddie, unabashed. "I'll put things right next time I see her."

But the sunshine had gone out of Morag's day. If Lord Toby had really been interested in her, he would not have reacted to the idea of her marrying Freddie the way he did. His green eyes had been hard, reflecting no emotion whatsoever. Until that moment, Morag had not realized she had clung on to a dream that Toby would disengage himself from Henrietta and marry her. She had been living in a fantasy world. Her head ached and all she wanted to do was lie down in a cool room.

". . . and Freemantle pays too much attention to what Rory says," she became aware Freddie was saying. "Bonapartiste spies, indeed."

"Take me home, Freddie," said Morag quietly. "I have the headache."

"Oh, very well," said Freddie, looking disappointed. He delivered her reluctantly into the hands of her butler, noting to himself that the fellow was overfamiliar for a servant and would have to go — as soon as they were married, of course.

Morag trailed up the stairs, nearly colliding with Rory, who was staggering down under the weight of his cat.

"Cannot that animal *walk?*" she demanded with some asperity.

"He *likes* being carried," said Rory hotly, springing to the defense of his beloved cat. "He killed three rats in the kitchen last night and cook and Hamish are extremely pleased with him. He is a resting warrior."

"Then I hope the resting warrior has not got fleas. Let me past, Rory. I must lie down."

"Are you going to marry Lord Freddie?" asked Rory, still blocking her path.

"No. I don't think so. I don't know."

"We don't need anyone else," said Rory earnestly. "We get on splendidly, just you and me and Mr. Service and The Beastie, of course."

The cat screwed its large head round to stare at Morag and gave her its sinister smile.

"Take that thing away. It gives me gooseflesh," said Morag. "Now, let me past, Rory. I do not want to marry *anyone*. Now what is it?" For Rory still barred her way.

"Astley's, mama," breathed Rory. "Mr. Service says, with your permission, he will take me to Astley's this evening."

Morag hesitated. She would, not so long ago, have refused point-blank. But look what had come of all her mollycoddling. "Very well," she said wearily. "Come to my room before you go. I wish to speak to Mr. Service so bring him with you."

What, after all, could be the harm in a visit to Astley's Amphitheatre? The shows were vulgar and spectacular, of that she had heard, but there was nothing dangerous about the place.

Rory danced off to tell Mr. Service the good news, the cat's heavy head jogging on his shoulder.

Hamish, however, was the first to hear the good news. The butler smiled tolerantly. He was still cautiously not overfond of Rory but a certain truce had been struck up between the two and the boy was a hundred times better since he had found that dreadful animal.

"I'll tell Mr. Service ye're going," smiled Hamish. "Go and wash your face and hands and change your clothes."

"Isn't it marvelous!" cried Rory. "I'm going to the Surrey side." The Surrey side of London was famous for its theatres, which catered to the more unsophisticated tastes. Of these, Astley's was the most famous, combining all the joys of the theatre with that of the circus.

"I heard a poem once about the Surrey side," said Hamish. "Gie me a bit time and I'll remember it. Ah, I have it now."

The butler began to recite carefully in precise English:

> "Can I forget those wicked lords,
> Their vices and their calves;
> The things they did upon those boards,
> And never did by halves;
> The peasant, brave though lowly born,
> Who constantly defied
> Those wicked lords with utter scorn,
> Upon the Surrey side!"

Rory laughed. This sort of poetry was more to his taste than any of his "mother's" volumes.

He spent the next hour getting ready. Then he tucked The Beastie up in his bed and kissed the top of its large head.

He ran to find Mr. Service and fairly pulled that large gentleman along to Morag's private sitting room.

There was no sign of her and Rory quietly pushed open the bedroom door. Morag was asleep. He hesitated. If he awoke her, she might regret her earlier decision. She might not let him go!

He decided to leave her a note instead.

He crossed to the writing desk in the corner of the sitting room and sat down. He was scribbling a note to explain that he had not wanted to awaken her when suddenly he at last put a face to that voice he had heard at Lady Montclair's. He quickly wrote down that piece of information, signed and sanded it.

"Come, Mr. Service," he said, putting his small hand confidently in the big man's. "We shall not wake my mother and, after all, there is no need. She has already given me permission to go."

Morag struggled up out of sleep, vaguely aware of diminishing voices in the corridor outside. She had meant to instruct Mr. Service to bring Rory straight home and not allow himself to be lured into Vauxhall Gardens, which was near Astley's, to watch the fireworks. But he was a sensible man, she thought, climbing slowly from bed, and could be trusted to take care of the boy.

She rang the bell for Scott, saying, "Lay out anything at all. I do not care what I wear this evening. I shall not be going out."

Nonetheless, she selected a pretty sprigged muslin gown. Would she never rid herself of the foolish hope of seeing Lord Toby Freemantle?

"There a note from his lordship," said Scott, handing her Rory's letter. "His lordship?" repeated Morag, her face lighting up.

"Yes, my lady. Master Rory."

"Oh!" Fighting down a twinge of disappointment, Morag scanned the schoolboyish scrawl with an indulgent smile on her face. Then she read the last two lines and turned white.

"Lord Freemantle, Scott. Send a footman for Lord Freemantle. We need help. Fetch Hamish!"

"It's Hamish's night off," said Scott. "Is there anything I can do?"

"Yes, yes," babbled Morag. "Get Lord Freemantle. Send two footmen — one to his address and one to his club."

"Lord Freemantle to see your ladyship," announced the footman from the doorway.

Lord Toby waited nervously in the drawing room. He had told Henrietta that he could not marry her. She had shrieked and ranted and raved and then to his relief had said that *he* was not breaking the engagement, *she* was. And that had been that! He was a free man. Now all he dreaded was that he might be too late — was she engaged to Lord Freddie? Surely not.

He rehearsed all sorts of speeches in his mind and tried to imagine the coming meeting, how she would look, what she would say.

But the reality was stranger than anything he could have imagined. She threw herself into his arms, crying, "Toby! Oh, it was Freddie all the time!"

"Oh, Mr. Service! I think you are *God!*" cried Rory, as he sat beside his large companion in

Astley's Amphitheatre.

" 'Ere now!" declared Mr. Service, looking profoundly shocked. "You h'aint ought to talk like that, young 'un. That's blasfeemissus. You sit there and stow it or I'll take you home."

"Yes, sir," said Rory meekly, although his eyes danced.

Was there ever such a place as Astley's!

He sat among all the paint and gilding and mirrors, facing a curtain which as yet hid all the mysteries of the theatre. In front of the curtain was a ring with clean white sand.

The orchestra was tuning up in that dilatory tuneless way of theatre orchestras — the most exciting sound in the world. They had had a tremendous fight to get in, what with the crowd heaving and jostling in front of the paybox. Mr. Service had coped with that by hoisting Rory onto his broad shoulders and using his fists to good effect. They soon had their checks and were able to battle their way in, well before the performance was due to start.

And then the curtains parted and the fun began.

It opened with a marvelous piece where the hero was shut up in a mill. He tried to escape up a ladder, only to find himself confronted by the ruthless villain, barring his escape with a horse pistol. How the audience hissed that villain! Then as the hero gave himself up for lost, a door higher up flew open to reveal the heroine, brandishing *two* horse pistols which she fired dramatically while the ladies of the audience screamed. The villain was confounded. Tableau and curtain where the villain bowed his thanks to a storm of boos and hisses.

Then there was a clown and a tall thin military man who made Rory and Mr. Service laugh so hard they thought they would burst.

" 'Ave a pint o' wet," said a hoarse voice at Mr. Service's elbow and he took it and swallowed it gratefully in one gulp. He turned to thank his new friend but the seat next to him was empty.

Meanwhile Rory was applauding a splendidly intelligent horse who had discovered the name of the murderer and who would not walk on all fours until the murderer was taken into custody but pranced around on its hind legs.

Then the first act ended with a beautiful lady who jumped over nine and twenty ribbons held out by the cast and came down safely on her horse's back. Rory cheered till he was hoarse and then turned his glowing face to Mr. Service.

But Mr. Service was slumped back on the bench, his chin on his chest, breathing heavily. Rory shook him.

"Wake up, Mr. Service!" he cried, tugging at his jacket. "You're going to miss all the fun." But his tutor's head was lolling on his chest. Rory saw the tankard dangling from Mr. Service's listless hand. Drunk! But he couldn't be. He had been as sober as anything only a minute ago.

He looked round for help. Mr. Service had

taken him to the cheaper seats rather than to a box, thinking that the boy would have more fun from mingling with the crowd. Then at the end of the row, Rory saw the cheerful, boyish features of Lord Freddie Rotherwood and crouched back in his seat. He had a sudden awful feeling that Lord Freddie's remarks at Lady Montclair's about being loyal to Napoleon had not been a joke. His wits sharpened with fear, he knew that Lord Freddie had come looking for him and that, in some peculiar way, he was responsible for Mr. Service's sleep. Then Lord Freddie turned and looked straight along the row at him. Rory sat paralyzed with fear. Freddie edged down toward him, his cheerful smile painted on his face.

"Well, surprise!" he cried. "What's happened to your gorilla? Drunk?"

"No," said Rory. "Drugged," and then he could have bitten his tongue out. Now Freddie knew that *he* knew what the game was. He should have played for time.

"As a matter of fact I came looking for you," said Freddie. "Your mother asked me to bring you home."

He sounded so frank and honest that Rory's spirits rose. But then they dropped just as quickly. He knew instinctively that however badly his mother wanted him home, she would never have made him leave in the middle.

"So let's go, laddie," Freddie was saying.

"No," said Rory. "You are not in charge of me.

Mr. Service is. I shall wait until he wakes up. So there!"

The smile left Freddie's face. He caught hold of Rory's arm in a painful grip. "Come along."

"Help!" screamed Rory suddenly. "This man is a French spy. He's going to kill me. Help!" The crowd looked, amazed, from Rory's contorted face to Freddie's open boyish one and some began to laugh. "Take 'im 'ome, guv," called a man. " 'e's bin seein' too much play'ouse."

Freddie sat down suddenly, pulling Rory with him. Rory felt something hard pressing against his side. "Feel that!" hissed Freddie. "That, dear boy, is the pistol with which I killed old Cosmo. Didn't want him around mucking up the family escutcheon or whatever it was he was holding over your mother. I'm going to marry your mother but you . . ." He broke off but Rory finished the sentence in his mind for him. "You won't be around to see it."

Rory was paralyzed with fright. He knew that Freddie was going to make sure he wasn't going to be around to tell anyone anything. He couldn't shoot him in the middle of Astley's? Oh, yes he could, thought Rory, remembering the piece in the mill and the loud bangs of the stage guns.

"You're joking, sir," said Rory, forcing himself to relax. "You shouldn't tease me like that. I tell you what. Let me see the end of the show and I'll go with you."

Freddie stared down at the boy in surprise and

Rory looked back at him with limpid gray-blue eyes. *He really does think I was joking,* thought Freddie. *He knows I'm a spy but he doesn't think I mean to murder him. Best sit still and await my chance. There should be some noise from the stage any moment now.*

To Rory's relief the first performer in the second act was a lady who rejoiced in the name of Kitty Pretty. She sang a sentimental ballad and, when that was over, shouted coyly out to the audience. "Who'll be my gallant?"

There was a roar of "me me" and Kitty flirted with her skirts. It was part of her act to select some man from the audience and bring him "on stage" — or rather the edge of the circus ring — and sing to him.

Rory grasped what it was she wanted and realized Freddie could not shoot him in full view of everyone.

"Me!" he yelled, his shrill, childish voice carrying over that of the men. "Me!" And before Freddie knew what he was about, Rory had wriggled along the bench, urged on by the cheering spectators and run to the edge of the gallery. "Me!" he cried.

Kitty Pretty peered up and saw the fair-haired child, waving frantically over the edge of the gallery. "Come on down, young 'un," she called.

Eager hands swung Rory over the balcony, more hands caught him and swung him down over the boxes and into the pit and thrust him forward toward Kitty.

Kitty was delighted with Rory. She began to sing her next song right into his face, a state of affairs which would normally have embarrassed Rory dreadfully, but as things were he stared adoringly up at Kitty. And then out of the corner of his eye, he saw Freddie walking through the pit toward him.

"Don't let him get me!" he cried to Kitty, who glared at him and went on singing.

They were standing in the middle of the white sand of the circus ring. Freddie marched coolly up. "Time I took this lad home," he said loudly, cutting Kitty off in mid-warble.

"Leave the boy alone," shouted a familiar voice. Rory let out a sob of relief and Lord Toby Freemantle strode into the ring, followed by Morag.

The orchestra trailed off into silence. Kitty looked desperately from Lord Freddie to Lord Toby to Rory, who was being clutched to the bosom of a beautiful red-headed girl, and then her face cleared. That idiot of a manager had staged this seemingly impromptu act without telling her. Well, she would show him that she was up to snuff. She remembered just such a scene in the *Wicked Baron*. She took a couple of fencing foils out of the prop basket in the corner and remembered her lines. "If you must fight," she cried, "at least fight like gentlemen."

The audience cheered and settled back to enjoy the show. For a moment, it had all looked serious but it was just one of Astley's stunts after all.

"Come quietly," Lord Toby was saying. "The authorities are already on their way here."

In answer, Freddie knocked the button off the end of his foil. "You're mad!" said Lord Toby, and in that moment, he realized Freddie was indeed mad. The boyish face seemed to have crumpled into a mask of ratlike cunning.

Freddie laughed and Lord Toby quickly parried. Then he knocked the button off his own foil. "Oh, Toby, be careful!" screamed Morag, still clutching Rory. The orchestra struck up a lively number.

The audience at Astley's really thought the acting was splendid. These two big bucks seemed genuinely out to kill each other and that pretty miss with the child was acting her heart out.

The two antagonists riposted, parried and feinted while the audience roared its appreciation. Both were fine swordsmen. Members of the Quality in the lower boxes assumed Lord Toby and Lord Freddie were doing it for a bet and promptly began to lay wagers themselves.

As the duel went on, a queer silence fell on the audience. It was all too real, the panting, striving men and the frightened girl and terrified child.

Both men were hampered by the fact that neither had had time to remove his jacket or boots and both their jackets were tailored to allow the minimum of movement.

Suddenly there was a commotion at the entrance of the theater and a group of the Bow

Street Horse Patrol marched down the aisle in their blue greatcoats and the red waistcoats which gave them the nickname of Robin Red-breasts.

Someone gave them a cheer but the rest of the audience suddenly knew that the scene in front of them was real. For they knew to a man that these were real officers of the law and not actors.

At that moment, Lord Toby broke through Freddie's guard and plunged his sword deep into Freddie's side. He pulled it out, wiping it on his jacket sleeve, and stood back as Freddie fell in the sawdust. Tableau. Hero stands over villain. Curtain. The audience went mad and cheered them to the echo. Now that it was all over, they felt sure it had been staged.

Chapter Thirteen

Lord Toby Freemantle was definitely *mauvais ton*. The fact that he had apprehended a murderer did not please the patronesses of Almack's one little bit. He should have done it in a more seemly manner, they said, instead of exhibiting himself before the vulgar gaze at Astley's. Henrietta told everyone and anyone who would listen what a narrow escape she had had — in increasingly shrill tones.

Lord Freddie confessed to the murders of Cosmo and Miss Simpson and then had hanged himself with his cravat in his cell — a sordid ending to a sordid affair. The military had ransacked his lodgings for evidence of state secrets and had only found evidence of poor Freddie's mad adoration of Napoleon.

The French actors were rounded up and questioned and one remembered the conversation at Lady Montclair's. Milord was quite mad, he said, and had been convinced he could rescue Napoleon. Freddie had apparently planned to marry Morag and use her fortune to bribe the necessary people to effect the emperor's escape.

Why had the French actor not reported Lord

Rotherwood to the authorities? The actor had given a Gallic shrug. Milord was definitely mad. Anyone could see that. He had paid him not the slightest attention.

"Why didn't I guess?" wailed Morag. "I even considered marrying him. And to think I told him about Cosmo and he went out and shot the poor laird just like that!"

This was said to Lord Toby Freemantle who was lounging in a corner of her drawing room and admiring her figure as she paced up and down.

"I haven't known which way to turn," went on Morag. "It has been two whole weeks since that dreadful evening and you did not call. Now the patronesses of Almack's have withdrawn my vouchers. I am *ruined*."

"They'll have forgotten the whole thing by next Season," said Lord Toby with cynical indifference. "Had I realized you were become a Nobody, I should certainly have called. I thought my unfashionable presence would ruin your Season."

"To leave me *alone* . . ." went on Morag angrily, but he interrupted her with, "Did you miss me?"

She stopped and stared at him, her mouth open.

"Ah, no!" she cried at last, her voice husky. "You are not to flirt with me, my lord. I am in no mood for dalliance."

He stood up and walked quickly over to her

and jerked her roughly into his arms. "I am not flirting. Listen to me! We will continue to shock society by proceeding north together where we will be married unfashionably over the anvil at Gretna. Dear Rory will stay with us until the end of summer when we will send him to Brown's seminary in the King's Road to cram for Eton which should keep his mischievous brain well occupied. Now, what do you say?"

"I-I c-can't . . ." she began so he kissed her, quite savagely and long until she had no breath left.

"Try again," he said, raising his mouth from hers.

"It's no use, Toby," sighed Morag. "There is something I have to tell you. No, leave me. Sit over there. Don't touch me until I've finished."

He saw that she was indeed serious so he did as he was bid. Morag studied him for a few moments as if to say good-bye. The square handsome face, those odd green eyes, the strong athletic figure shown, at the moment, to its best advantage in a pair of skintight Inexpressibles, a pair of shiny Hessian boots with little gold tassels, a blue swallowtail coat and an intricately tied cravat.

Morag began in a faltering but determined voice to tell him of her lack of success as a marriage partner to the earl. "So you see," she finished, looking away, "you will find that there is something repellent in me."

Hamish pressed his ear to the drawing room

door, the sweat running down his face. He wanted his mistress to marry Lord Toby more than anything. Furthermore, he wanted to go home. He seriously considered bursting in and telling Morag the truth — that the earl would have been the same with any gently bred girl. But grateful though he might be, Lord Toby would never forgive him for such familiarity.

Then he heard Lord Toby's great shout of laughter. "Oh, my foolish love," he cried, sweeping Morag up in his arms and striding to the doors of the drawing room. "We are going to lay your fears to rest."

Holding her tightly with one arm Lord Toby reached down to the door handle. But the doors were promptly thrown open and Hamish stood there, executing a low bow.

Toby raised his eyebrows in faint surprise but nonetheless marched past toward the stairs, holding Morag as tightly as he could.

"What are you doing with my mother?" came a sharp, imperative, childish voice. Rory stood blocking the stairs, his eyes snapping with jealousy.

"She needs to lie down," said Toby calmly.

At that moment, Hamish saw The Beastie trundling slowly across the hall and quickly scooped it up, opened the door to the kitchens and threw the animal down the stairs where it let out a loud yell.

"Beastie!" cried Rory, his attention immediately diverted. He shot past Morag and Lord

Toby and vanished down the steps to the kitchens.

"Put me down, Toby!" cried Morag as he kicked open the door of her bedroom. "What will the servants think?"

"To hell with the servants!" said Lord Toby Freemantle, kicking the door shut behind them.

Down in the kitchen, Rory was murmuring sweet nothings to his cat. Having assured himself that the animal had come to no harm, he turned purposefully toward the door again — to find his way blocked by Hamish and Mr. Service. Mr. Service was now as fanatically loyal a retainer as Hamish, having been overwhelmed at the magnanimity of Lady Murr for having kept him in her employ despite the fact that he had allowed himself to be tricked at Astley's like the veriest greenhorn.

"And where do you think you're going?" demanded Mr. Service, who had been in hasty consultation with Hamish.

"I am going to see my mother," said Rory with a glint in his eye that reminded Hamish of the Rory of pre-cat days. "I fear she may wed Lord Toby Freemantle and, although he is very well in his way, we are quite happy without my mother becoming married."

"If your mither disnae get marrit," said Hamish slowly, "then you'll never get tae school. It's Lord Toby's idea that ye should cram for Eton come this autumn."

Eton! Other boys. And books, books, books.

"You mean it?" breathed Rory.

"Aye," grinned Hamish. "But we're goin' hame tae Perth first. I've been thinkin', ye ken thon tree? The one you said you liked tae climb?"

Rory nodded.

"Well, I could help ye build a wee house up in the branches. You could play up there with The Beastie."

"Oh, Hamish, truly?" cried Rory.

"Yes, truly. Now if you wash your hands over at the sink there, Mr. Service and me is going out for a walk and we ken a good sweetie shop round the corner, so . . ."

Rory scampered to the sink and Hamish mopped his brow. Master Rory was going to be taken for a very long walk indeed. Long enough for Lord Toby to persuade the mistress to marry him.

"You'll have to marry me now," Lord Toby said smiling down at her. "My dear delight, you were made for love. Are all your fears at rest?"

"Except for one," said Morag, a small frown creasing her brow. "Rory."

"I will adopt him. What else?"

"Are we . . . I mean, am I . . . doing a dreadful thing by cheating Lord Arthur out of his inheritance?"

"No," he said gently, smoothing the frown away with one long finger. "The earl was sensible, you know. Arthur would be a bad landlord. Think of all your tenants and how many farms would be mortgaged across the gaming tables of St. James's. Furthermore, if you had all the bastards in the top ten thousand exposed, my dear heart, the British aristocracy would fall to rack and ruin."

Morag opened her mouth again and he closed it with a kiss.

"It is getting late," said Rory fretfully, "and my feet hurt."

Hamish pulled out a large turnip watch and then winked at Mr. Service over the boy's head.

"I bring to mind," said Mr. Service, clearing his throat, "that Madame Saqui is to walk the slack wire at Vauxhall tonight. Perhaps 'er ladyship might give this 'ere limb permishun for to go."

"Aye, it's a fine sight that," said Hamish. "But it means the lad would be out ower late. Still, it's worth seein', Rory. She walks up there above the crowds with all the Golden Drops and Bengal Lights flashing around her."

"Oh, please let me go! Please take me!" cried Rory, his sore feet forgotten. "I will not complain. I will do anything. Only persuade my mother to let me go."

"Ah, well," grinned Hamish. "My leddy's probably restin' so we'll leave a wee note on the hall table. Dinnae fash yersel', my lord. My leddy won't worry about you this night."

"You called me 'my lord' for the first time," said Rory, staring up at the butler.

"Oh, aye, so I did," said Hamish, tucking the boy's hand in his own and smiling down at him. "So I did!"

We hope you have enjoyed this Large Print book. Other G.K. Hall & Co. or Chivers Press Large Print books are available at your library or directly from the publishers.

For more information about current and upcoming titles, please call or write, without obligation, to:

G.K. Hall & Co.
P.O. Box 159
Thorndike, Maine 04986 USA
Tel. (800) 257-5157

OR

Chivers Press Limited
Windsor Bridge Road
Bath BA2 3AX
England
Tel. (0225) 335336

All our Large Print titles are designed for easy reading, and all our books are made to last.